Beautiful Forever

Kendall Ryan is the *New York Times* and *USA Today* bestselling author of contemporary romance novels, including *Hard to Love*, *Unravel Me*, *Resisting Her* and the *Filthy Beautiful Lies* series.

She's a sassy, yet polite Midwestern girl with a deep love of books, and a slight addiction to lipgloss. She lives in Minneapolis with her adorable husband and two baby sons, and enjoys cooking, hiking, being active, and reading. Find out more at www.kendallryanbooks.com

Also by Kendall Ryan

FILTHY
Beautiful Forever

Kendall Ryan

BOOK 4

HARPER

Harper
An imprint of HarperCollins*Publishers*
1 London Bridge Street
London SE1 9FG

www.harpercollins.co.uk

A Paperback Original 2015
1

A catalogue record for this book
is available from the British Library

ISBN: 978-0-00-813392-4

Set in Minion by Born Group using Atomik ePublisher from Easypress

MIX
Paper from
responsible sources

FSC
www.fsc.org

FSC™ C007454

Chapter One

Collins

I can't seem to ejaculate lately.

It isn't from lack of effort on my part. Hell, no. I'm no quitter, but despite pumping into my very hot supermodel girlfriend for the last hour, trying every position you can imagine, and even inventing a few of my own, I am nowhere near coming.

Fuck.

Sweat drips from my abs and chest onto hers, and I murmur an apology and thrust harder, slamming into her body again and again as I try to get there. She's already come four times and during her last two orgasms she asked me if I was close. Yes, I lied.

Giving a final huff, she pushes me off her. 'What the hell, Collins?' She moves from the bed, tossing a pillow at my face, as she grabs her silk robe.

I sit back on my heels; naked as the day I was born, wondering what the fuck is wrong with me. Tatianna is tall and thin with long silky hair, and she's front and center in the mental spank banks of men worldwide. This has nothing to do with her, or shit, maybe it does, I don't know.

'Listen, babe, I'm just tired, okay?' I'd run six miles that morning and then done a brutal kickboxing workout with my youngest brother, Pace. And hell, maybe some of the conversation we'd had while throwing jabs and uppercuts is still spinning in my head. When he'd inquired about my relationship with Tatianna, I'd admitted to him that I was pretty sure she only regarded me as her personal bank account, and she was merely a warm body to lose myself in. Only that isn't working so well for me lately either.

I watch from the bed as Tatianna dresses herself, choosing designer garments from the massive walk-in closet I had built for her. She tosses stray clothes to the floor before finally settling on a black shift dress and matching heels. 'I'm going out,' she says in my direction.

I know she's pissed at me, but shouldn't we talk about this? Isn't that what couples do?

I merely nod.

I'm sure she's going out shopping, her typical Saturday after-noon activity.

After she's gone, I shower and dress, then sit alone in the library enjoying a one-hundred year old scotch. I consider calling my brothers, but they're probably each busy with their families. Leaning back in the leather armchair, I close my eyes.

I exercise control over all things in my life—from my company, to my relationships, to the way I handle my business—only my cock hasn't gotten the memo. The selfish prick.

I could make an appointment for a physical—but I'm sure my doctor would tell me the problem is with my head, not my dick. I can come just fine with my own hand—and I don't want to hear why he thinks that is. *Not something I care to examine, thanks, Doc.*

As the oldest brother in a family without a mother, and a father who worked too much, a hell of a lot fell on my shoulders. I ran a tight ship and made sure my brothers kept in line. And now, as the CEO of a company, it's no different. I rarely have time for frivolous things, like fun. Maybe now I'm paying the price. I've forgotten how to fucking ejaculate. *Christ.*

I'm sitting alone, enjoying a drink while the sun sinks low in the sky, when the doorbell chimes. No one rings the bell. My brothers would let themselves in, and the housekeepers would enter through the garage. I push up from the chair and head toward the foyer, wondering who the hell is at my front door.

I open the door to find a young woman standing on my front porch. There's something alluring and vaguely familiar about her wide set mossy-colored eyes fringed in dark lashes. My dick perks up in interest. *Really, now?* To this brown haired girl who looks equal parts terrified and hopeful?

We each stand there, eyes roaming over the other. Did her car break down? It seems unlikely that she hiked the mile up my private driveway. I'm about to offer her my cell phone when she speaks for the first time.

'Collins?' She squints at me, like she isn't just looking at me, but looking *into* me, as strange as that sounds. Her voice has a familiar quality to it. Soft, yet gravelly. My memory scrambles through a scotch-induced haze to place her.

'Gremlin? Is that you?' I find that I'm the one squinting now, trying to understand how the girl I used to know by that nickname has transformed into this beautiful creature before me.

'It's Mia now,' she corrects me with a pout.

'Mia, fuck!' I pull her into my arms, squeezing her against my chest. She's still the same height as when we were teens—barely clearing five feet, whereas I've sprouted up to a commanding six-foot-two.

Her posture relaxes once she's in my arms and she lets out a small chuckle. 'I didn't think you recognized me at first.'

'I've had a lot on my mind today. Besides you look just a little different than the last time I saw you.' I release her and meet her eyes, and I can tell we're both remembering the last time we were together. We were fifteen years old and below deck on my dad's boat while it swayed gently at the dock. She'd told me that she was moving. And then begged me to take her virginity. Which I did. My last memory of her is with blood smears on her thighs and tears blurring her emerald green eyes. I still feel like a shit for that night. Shame burns hotly through me, forcing me back into the present.

I clear my throat, and Mia blinks away the memories no doubt clouding her vision. If she's here on my doorstep in LA, maybe that means she's forgiven me for that night. We grew up together and were pretty much inseparable from the time we were five years old. Until she moved away. I haven't seen or spoken to her in fifteen years. As I drink in her appearance, I realize some things are still the same—her green eyes that sparkle when they catch the light and her messy brown hair that curls every which way, but some other things are definitely new. Those tits for instance. I'd remember those. Her waist is tapered and trim, but her hips flare out, and without needing her to turn around, I can tell her ass is round and lush. The girl has curves that are completely at odds with the scrawny, scab-kneed tomboy I recall playing with my entire childhood.

'What are you doing in LA?' I ask.

'I…' She pulls in a deep breath. 'It's a long story. Can I come in?'

'Of course.' I'd been practically guarding the door like a jackass. I step aside and welcome her in. She has a large suitcase with her, and I offer to take it, pulling it inside and leaving it by the front door, since I have no idea what its presence means.

'Your home is amazing,' she says, her eyes darting up the curved staircase that rises above us.

'Thank you,' I murmur. I don't want to talk about my home, I want to understand why she's here. The mischievous twinkle in her eyes has dimmed, and even though I haven't seen her in fifteen long years, I hate the thought that something happened to her. This woman once meant everything to me.

I show her around, giving her a brief tour of the first floor before leading her into the library. My drink is still on the side table, reminding me of my shitty afternoon. 'Would you like one?' I ask.

'Sure,' she says. 'But only if you have something a bit less manly than whatever that is.' She waves her hand at the glass of amber-colored liquor.

'I think I can make that happen.' I head to the small bar in the corner of the room, and pour some vodka into a glass, then reach into the mini-fridge below and grab cans of lemon-lime soda and cranberry juice. 'Will this work?' I ask, holding them up for her approval.

She nods and smiles at me. It was always so easy to make her happy.

I hand her the pink drink, and she joins me, sitting down in the leather armchair across from mine.

Seeing her here, watching her cross her ankles, and the delicate way she brings the glass to her lips...it evokes all kinds of memories.

Our relationship had never been romantic—we were friends—best friends. But when I lost my mom tragically in an auto accident at age fourteen, it was Mia who was there for me. It was Mia who I wanted. For days I couldn't eat, wouldn't talk to anyone, not even my brothers. I remember Mia holding me with my head against her chest. I listened to her heartbeat while she stroked my hair and told me silly little stories to distract me. The pain was so all-encompassing, so deep, I didn't know how to put it into words. But Mia didn't need words. She knew.

It was after one of those sessions that we shared our first kiss. It felt natural with none of the fumbling, over-zealous tongue attacks that some of my previous partners had. I'd instantly grown hard for my friend, and that confused the shit out of me. I'd never seen her as more until that moment. But something changed that night, because from that day on, I began noticing her as a developing woman. I would catch her watching me too, her eyes following me around the room with a certain curiosity twinkling in their green depths.

It was about a year after my mom's passing when she told me she had something important to tell me, and we agreed to meet late one night out on my dad's boat.

It sat in its slip at the dock, and while there was no sign of Mia, I climbed below deck, surprised to find she was already there waiting for me on the pullout bed. I crawled up beside her, the moon our only source of light. With a solemn expression, she told me that her parents were moving across the state, and that they couldn't afford to send her to private school anymore.

I remember my stomach twisting into a knot, and pulling her close to me. I couldn't stand the idea of her leaving. Needing to fix it, to take away Mia's tears, I'd called my father on his cell phone right then. I asked him about paying for her schooling so she could remain at Linden Academy, but he'd blown me off. He said there would be other girls and I shouldn't give my heart away at age fifteen. But he didn't know that I'd given her my heart the day we met. We were five years old, and I still remember the first time I laid eyes on her. She was so small, much smaller than all the other kindergarteners and was being bullied by a couple of the older kids. Unable to stomach the thought of someone so defenseless being hurt, I rushed to her side. The big green eyes that latched onto mine pierced straight through me, and the silly smile that uncurled on her mouth did me in. She'd captured a piece of me that day.

When I hung up with my father, the look in Mia's eyes told me she already knew his answer. But the next words out of her mouth shocked the shit out of me. She told me she was a virgin, which I assumed, and said she wanted me to be her first.

God, just thinking of that conversation transports me back to that humid July night. My stomach was rolling with nerves, and even though I knew we probably shouldn't, my dick was rock hard at the thought of fucking her. At being inside her first.

Hoping she didn't look down and notice the erection straining in my gym shorts, I told her we couldn't. We weren't even dating, and with her leaving the next day, I was worried she'd regret it, and I didn't want her to feel bad after. She said she didn't want it to be with anyone else and wanted to always have the memory of her first time being with me. She made a very convincing argument, or hell, maybe I didn't need much convincing.

I only agreed to do it because I made her promise that she would be okay when she left the next day. She promised me she'd move on, accept her move, and date other guys at her new high school. I believed her.

I gave her one slow kiss, pressing my lips against hers, giving her the chance to change her mind and pull away. Only she didn't. Her tongue licked against my lower lip, and when I opened, it slipped inside my mouth and stroked mine.

Mia was surprised that I didn't have a condom with me. She assumed I'd done it with a few of the girls from school that I'd messed around with. When I admitted it would be my first time too, she looked at me like she understood that we were both giving a piece of ourselves to the other. I jogged up to my house and retrieved a condom, and was back at the boat within minutes. I was guessing that by the time I made it back, she would have changed her mind, but instead she was undressed and under the quilt, quietly waiting for me with wide green eyes.

I still remember the tight squeeze of her around my cock, the puff of breath against my neck when I fully entered her, the way it felt when I came inside the latex for the first time, wiping her clean after and worrying that she hadn't come. My chest gets tight as feelings of lust mix with ones of shame. I fucked up that night.

'Collins?' she asks, pulling me from my faraway thoughts.

I clear my throat. 'Sorry. It's just surreal seeing you here. Tell me what brought you to LA. Are you still living in Connecticut?' I ask. I hate the formality of my questions, but we have lost ground to cover, and the scared look on her face when I'd opened the door is still lingering in my mind.

She takes a big gulp of her drink. 'This is going to sound crazy…' she laughs nervously.

'Mia, I've known you since you were five. We used to tell each other everything.'

I didn't know if someone had hurt her…or if she was running from something, but I waited patiently while she gathered her courage and downed several more sips of her drink.

'Remember that promise we made each other?' she says.

I watch her quietly. She was going to have to be more specific. Shit, it'd been fifteen years. 'About?' I probe.

'Us. When we turned thirty…' She swallows nervously.

I take a deep breath, trying to understand where she is headed with this. 'Mia?'

'When we were ten. We promised each other that if neither of us was married by the time we were thirty, we'd marry each other.'

The memory drifts into my head. Her soulful green eyes looking up at me like I was her savior, our pinky's locking together in solidarity. Christ, we had promised that, hadn't we? The suitcase by the front door. The fact that I'd turned thirty a few months ago. All of it slams into me at once, and a panicky feeling presses against my chest.

Heels clicking across the wood floor capture our attention. 'There you are,' Tatianna says, entering the library. 'This house is really too big.' She takes in Mia's presence and stops. 'Oh, I'm sorry, I assumed you were alone. Hi, I'm Tatianna.' She holds out her hand and Mia rises to her feet and shakes it.

'Mia. It's nice to meet you. I'm sorry, I should go...' She sets down her drink.

I rise to my feet and place my hands against Mia's shoulders. 'You don't have to go anywhere. I'm sure it's been a long day of traveling. Please sit.'

She swallows and watches me uneasily. 'Are you sure?'

I nod. 'Very. It sounds like we have a lot of catching up to do.' After that fucking bomb she just dropped on me, there's no way she's going anywhere.

She nods, her smile unsure.

'Tatianna, would you like to join us for a drink?' I ask, heading to the bar.

'Sure,' she says, her voice flat.

I make her the raspberry vodka-soda mixture she likes and hand her the glass. Tatianna sits down across the room and crosses her legs, her posture straight as a rod and her eyes glaring blankly ahead. She's still pissed about earlier.

I fill Mia in on the past fifteen years—that my brothers and I all live in the Los Angeles area now and that I run a successful investment firm downtown. My mouth is saying the words, but my brain is still trying to wrap around the fact that she showed up here after all these years.

Both women watch me and listen, Mia interjecting with questions every now and then, laughing happily when I tell her both of my younger brothers are settled down—Pace with a young son and Colton just got married last month.

Mia doesn't offer many details about her life, or what has prompted her to come here, but I'm guessing Tatianna's presence has thrown her off. There is still a lot I want to know.

'So, I'm sorry,' Tatianna interrupts, 'who did you say you were?'

'Mia was my best friend growing up,' I answer for her, not liking Tatianna's tone.

'Yes. We were pretty much inseparable until we were fifteen.'

'What happened when you were fifteen?' Tatianna asks, not knowing the minefield she's walking into.

My eyes lock on Mia's and her cheeks heat. I can tell she's remembering our first and only sexual encounter. I still worry that I'd been too rough with her. The way her small body trembled in my arms after, the blood I saw between her legs. I feel sick just thinking about it. If I had the chance to redo things today, I'd fuck her so well, she'd never want to leave. Christ, did my brain take a sick day too? I need to lock it up. Mia is not here to fuck. I repeat the mantra in my head.

'My family moved,' Mia answers, blinking and looking away from me. 'And you are?' Mia asks, and takes a sip of her drink.

Tatianna frowns at me, obviously not happy that I hadn't offered up this information. 'I'm his girlfriend.'

Chapter Two

Mia

'I'm his girlfriend,' Tatianna says. She's answering *my* question, but her glare is directed at *Collins*.

I'm mid sip, and her admission makes me suck in a breath—or drink rather—down the wrong way, sending me into a coughing fit.

'Excuse me,' I stammer between coughs. 'I'm sorry. Of course you are.' I manage to get my breathing back under control, but I can tell my face is flushed. Embarrassed isn't a strong enough word for how I feel. He has a girlfriend!? I want to die.

I think back to when he gave me the tour of his home. The place is amazing and beautifully decorated, but there were no photos of him with a woman, no flowers or feminine touches anywhere. There wasn't even a cozy nook where a girl might curl up and read a book or fashion magazine. And when Tatianna showed up, sure they were familiar with each other, but not in any way that even hinted at romance. Their eyes didn't linger on one another's, and from how far apart they sat, I just assumed she was an employee. Heck, the house is big enough that he must have several employees living here.

Also, I'd been so lost, deep in conversation with Collins, that I'd hardly noticed how beautiful she was. Now that I really look at her for the first time, it is obvious this is the type of woman he would

11

date. She's tall, slender and gorgeous. In fact, she looks familiar. I realize that she's Tatianna Markov, the woman whose photo was on the cover of every Vogue magazine I saw at the airport kiosk.

My stomach sinks as I look at both of them—a tricky feat since they are on opposite ends of the room. But while my gaze floats between them I see some familiar mannerisms. Both have matching perfect posture. Just looking at them makes me sit up straighter. Their faces are harsh and cool with neutral expressions that give nothing away. That's a new look for Collins. He never used to look so cold. I think back to our younger years. He was always guy-serious, but it was easy to put a smile on his face, one of my favorite things to do. The look on his face now is stern and immobile. I'm glad it isn't directed at me, but it's sad to see him this way at all.

Tatianna tosses her hair back and turns to me. 'So, what brings you to Los Angeles?'

My eyes dart to Collins, but he manages to hold his stoic look, unfazed by her question. In a panic, I try to take a sip of my drink but it's empty.

Collins gets up. 'I'll get you another one.' He steps over to the bar and sets up three more glasses, making another round for each of us.

I take a deep breath, anything to stall. I don't like lying, but there is no way I'm going to tell this woman I came here in the hopes of marrying her boyfriend. It was so stupid of me to come. I wish I'd taken time to think about what I was doing instead of just rushing online to find the cheapest ticket. It hadn't even occurred to me that he might not be single. Although I've always been a bit out of control whenever Collins was involved. Why should now be any different?

But I'm not going to share any of this with Tatianna. She would just laugh me out of the house if I did that. Her eyes are on me, waiting for me to respond.

'I...' I search for words, anything that isn't the real reason I came. 'I lost my job.' I feel myself sinking down in my chair, unable to believe I'm about to admit to Collins and his girlfriend that I am a failed accountant. 'I was fired actually.' *Someone please shut me up.*

Collins hands me a new drink, and I take several fortifying sips.

'What did you do?' he asks. He looks genuinely perplexed as he takes the seat across from me. I'm sure the girl he remembers never would have been careless enough to get fired from a job. I guess things change.

'I was an accountant.' I look down at my drink, stirring it with the straw. 'My boss framed me for embezzling funds. And I had no way to prove it.'

Collins holds his hand up as if to stop me. 'There's always a way. I know several excellent forensic accountants. I could help connect you with one.' He leans forward in his chair.

The concern in his eyes tells me he'll help me if I want. He'd always been protective of me, and I love seeing that side of him again. I chew the inside of my lip, considering it briefly, but I'm too humiliated by the whole thing, besides, it isn't worth the trouble. It was a small enough amount that they didn't press charges. I wave him off. 'It's not worth it. He only managed to get a couple thousand before he...or, rather 'I' was caught.'

Tatianna laughs. 'The guy must suck at embezzling if he only managed a few thousand.'

I force a smile, but a few thousand seems like a lot to me. They kept my last paycheck to make up for the loss. It would have been enough for me to at least pay rent for a few more months.

'Anyway, I'm here because I needed a place to get a fresh start.' I stir my drink as I try to think of any topic of conversation other than my failed accounting career.

Tatianna yawns and stretches in a way that looks more practiced than real. She's definitely *not* an actress.

I take it as a not so subtle suggestion that it's time for me to leave. Humiliated, I stand up, 'I should get going,' I say, downing the last of my drink, and placing it on the nearest table. I head out to the hall and the direction I hope will lead to my bag and the exit. I may not have enough money for more than one night in a hotel, but I can't stay here.

'Wait, Gremli...Mia. Hang on, where are you going?' Collins follows me out into the hallway, and catches my arm, forcing me to stop. The contact of his large hand closing around my upper arm sends chills zipping down my body. It's been a long time since he touched me so intimately, yet my body recalls that night with perfectly clarity.

'I shouldn't have come. You've got...' I wave my hand around vaguely, not sure what I'm referring to exactly. It could be the amazing house, beautiful girlfriend, or perfect life. Any one of these makes me feel small, but the combination makes me feel as if I could cry. I swallow against the hard lump in my throat and force myself to look up at him.

He smiles, making me smile.

'Nonsense. You came all this way. I want you to stay. At least a few days. We have *fifteen* years to catch up on.' His eyes latch onto mine, kind yet insistent. It makes me warm. He still has the look that makes me feel like I'm the only one who matters. How does he manage to do that, even while dating the drop-dead gorgeous woman in the next room? I don't know, but I can't say no to him. Not when he looks at me this way. Besides, the house is so big he must have ten extra bedrooms, it's not like I'm putting him out or anything.

I sigh. 'Okay.' Just thinking about a bed makes me tired. It was a long day and a long flight. A yawn escapes.

He leans back into the library doorway. 'I'm gonna give Gremlin here the purple bedroom.'

'Who? ...Whatever,' Tatianna answers in a dull tone.

He slides his hand around mine, as if we're still little kids, only now his hand is much larger, and my fingers and palm are swallowed by his firm grip. It feels completely natural, him taking my hand, and I follow him to the front hall where he effortlessly lifts my suitcase and pulls it up the steps. We venture down a long hallway until he finally stops in front of a door, opens it, and puts my suitcase down just inside.

'Grem...Mia, I'm glad you're here.' His mouth hooks up in a playful smirk as if he thinks it's funny that he can't seem to call me by my real name. The first time we met, I was wearing a Gremlins T-shirt. The outdated, thrift store tee was the reason he'd had to save me that first day in kindergarten. Some of the other kids were teasing me about my second-hand clothing, and he came to my rescue. After he told the other kids off, he managed to turn the whole thing into a joke by saying gremlins were cool, then calling me gremlin. Not in a mean way, but as friendly jab. I was so thankful for the rescue that he could have called me almost anything that day, and I would have laughed for him. The nickname unfortunately stuck.

I smile. It is kind of funny. But I also blush because we're alone again. Just the two of us, and he's looking at me in that way, again. The way he did when he first realized who I was at the front door. I had no way to be sure, but his eyes smoldered as if he was remembering our first and only time together, fifteen years ago on the boat.

I remembered that night as if it happened yesterday. I'd been so nervous, but so sure it was the right thing, and the only way to really say goodbye to him. It was a way for me to give him a part of me that he would have forever. He tried to talk me out of it, even though I could tell by the way his eyes surveyed my body that he wanted to devour me. I was so relieved when he finally

15

agreed, and also admitted that it was his first time too. Because it meant he also wanted me to have a part of him. A part I've held dear all these years.

He'd been so gentle, and so careful with me. I can't say he was perfectly smooth, but neither was I. Still, his kisses were warm, and his arms held me close as we struggled to figure out the best way to do what neither of us really knew how to do. But then he'd taken control, laying me down and moving over me. He had been so tender and so attentive; easing in slowly and making sure he didn't hurt me. Making sure I was okay. And it did hurt, but only a pinch and only for a moment. And then it was amazing. The feeling of having him inside me, filling me. The memory still makes me blush. And yet afterwards he was so worried he'd hurt me. I felt whole, so completely cared for.

But now, I'm thirty. And single. And jobless. And perhaps I'm crazy, but I want to recapture a bit of my youth – and the best part of it was him. Even though I pushed it out of my head for many years, as I grew older, I longed to share my life with someone. Not just someone. *Him. Collins.* My first love. My first everything. Deep down, my heart knew what my body felt all those years ago – we were destined to be together. I didn't know how or why, but I knew he'd eventually come back into my life when the time was right. I couldn't help but wonder if I purposefully avoided serious relationships all these years, avoiding commitment in order to fulfill our promise to each other. Every man I dated over the past decade was compared to him, and not a single one measured up. As embarrassed as I was to just show up on his doorstep unannounced, the boy I longed for all these years is now a man. And my body takes notice, my heart pumping hard as he watches me.

Now Collins is taller, and though still trim, his shoulders are broad like an Olympic swimmer. His cheekbones and jaw line matured and sharpened, and his once slender, soft lips have filled in, making them that much more lickable. Collins always stood tall and confident. His tailored, button up navy shirt is just loose enough to leave a bit to my imagination, and my imagination does naughty things with his beautiful abs.

He clears his throat.

My eyes drift up the blue shirt, which brings out the sparkle in his cool blue eyes.

'I don't want you to get to upset over Tatianna. She'll be fine with you staying here.'

I nod. 'Sure.' I doubt that, but I won't argue.

'There are fresh towels in your bathroom. If you need me, my bedroom is at the end of the hall.' There's a pause and he smiles, making his eyes sparkle. 'It's great to see you again.' He leans in and picks me up in a hug that is reminiscent of so many things. Our childish youth, our strong friendship, and our romantic farewell all those years ago. I know I shouldn't let myself feel so attached to him after only an hour, but the thought of watching him turn and walk away into the arms of Natasha, or Tatianna, or whatever the hell her name was makes me want to rip out my earrings and prepare myself for a full on girl fight.

After several long moments, where I can feel his heart beating against mine, he sets me down and closes the door, leaving me alone in the room.

I turn and lean my back against the door staring blankly at the guestroom and wonder what I'm really doing here.

Chapter Three

Collins

The door to the guestroom closes and I just stand there, still in shock that Mia is inside. That she's flown all the way to LA. And more surprising than anything is the fact she's still single after all these years. Not that it matters—I'm with Tatianna. But still, my heart feels full seeing her again. I've often wondered where she was, what she was doing. Shit, I figured she was married with a couple of kids by now.

I hated hearing that she'd been wrongly framed and then fired from her job. Although the accounting job made sense. She was always good with numbers. In the various childhood ventures I'd started, she'd always point out my mathematical errors. Funny, considering I owned one of the top investment firms on the West Coast.

I wander back downstairs, but Tatianna isn't in the library where I left her. The house feels cold and quiet. I head back upstairs to the master suite that takes up the entire second floor west wing.

'Tatianna?' I call, not finding her in the bedroom.

'In here,' she says from the *Hers* walk-in closet.

I find her hanging up clothes on little pink padded hangers. There are a half dozen shopping bags at her feet, and I'm reminded of our fight this afternoon. 'Are you okay?' I ask.

She stops what she's doing and watches me. 'Who is that woman?'

'Mia? She's a childhood friend.'

'You never dated her, did you?' Tatianna raises her manicured brows at me.

'No.' *Not officially.* 'We were close growing up, but her family moved across the state just before we started high school. Does it bother you that she's staying here?'

She shrugs. 'No, I guess not.'

'Come here.' I open my arms and Tatianna drops the garment she's holding to the carpet and steps into my arms. 'I'm sorry about earlier,' I whisper, placing my lips against her neck.

She sighs heavily and rests against me. 'It's okay. I know you have a lot on your mind with the merger and everything.'

The merger? That was three months ago. I don't correct her. 'It looks like you found some good things on today's outing, huh?' There are shopping bags and tissue paper littering the closet floor.

She nods. 'Bergman's was having a sample sale and then my favorite jewelry designer previewed their fall collection at the Grove today, so I swung down there.' I listen as she tells me about her day, my thoughts faraway. 'I'm just going to finish putting all this away, okay?'

I nod. She loves organizing her closet, and I know she can spend hours in there. I had it designed just how she wanted—with a brightly lit crystal chandelier hanging overhead, a floor-to-ceiling mirror on one wall and rows and rows of colorful high heeled shoes resting on the shelving at the end of the room.

I'm still too keyed-up to relax, so I head into the sitting room linked to the master suite and pull out my cell phone. I try to figure out which of my brothers to call while Tatianna hums quietly in the other room.

While I'm sure Pace remembers Mia, he's five years younger, and his memories of her will be spotty at best. Colton, then.

'You'll never guess who showed up here today,' I say in place of a greeting.

'A strippergram?' he asks.

'No.' I chuckle. 'Mia Monroe.'

It takes him only a second. 'No shit?'

'Yeah.'

We each wait silently on the phone. He knew how close we were growing up. Which means he knows how much she meant to me.

'Explain,' he says, finally. 'What's she been up to all this time? How does she look? Why is she there?' He shoots the questions off one after the other.

'She looks incredible.' I don't know why those are the first words out of my mouth. Probably because the image of her standing on my front porch is burned into my brain. Gone is the slender, boyish frame of youth, and in its place are generous curves and the soft rounded flesh of womanhood. 'She's an accountant now.' I don't mention that she'd been fired or the secret marriage promise we made when we were ten that she's come to collect on—because that's crazy. It's completely fucking nuts. And it makes my heart thump like it's got some type of damn tick. Maybe I should schedule that stupid physical after all.

'You still have a thing for her?' he surprises me by asking next.

'Of course not.' *Fuck.* 'I'm with Tatianna.'

He sighs, and I hear him tell Sophie that he'll be there in a few minutes. 'Yes, but we both know that Tatianna is just a convenience. You've been in love with Mia since you were five years old for fuck's sake.'

'I'm not in love with Mia,' I drop my voice. Tatianna does not need to hear this. Besides, I don't have time for love right now. It's messy and unpredictable. I don't do messy, or unpredictable. Never have. Wasn't about to start now. No fucking thank you.

'Well, now that she's back, the least you can do is man up and fuck her finally.' He laughs.

'Uh, already taken care of.'

'Fuck, man. She's only been there a couple of hours, and you've already banged her?'

'No, dumbshit. When we were fifteen. We were each other's first.' I have no idea why I'm telling him this information. I guess Mia's shocking entrance back into my life has brought out my sharing side.

'No shit?' he says. 'I always thought Erika Garcia sophomore year was your first.'

'No. It was Mia,' I say. 'On Dad's boat.'

'Interesting. I always took girls there too.'

'I know you did, you little horn dog. But I thought of it first.'

'Damn, Mia Monroe,' he says again.

'So what should I do?' I ask.

'Listen, all I'm saying is that I know you were crazy about her. I'm glad she's back in your life. Shit, I remember the year she moved. It was like someone took the spark out of you. Like they pulled the beating heart right out of your chest. You moped around for six months. Maybe this is a good thing. You can have some fun for once.'

'Fun? You're one to talk.' Actually, Sophie being in his life has been a game-changer. He's like a different man now. Much more light-hearted and easier going than before.

'I'm doing just fine, asshole. Worry about yourself,' he barks.

Maybe he's right. There's no reason that he and Pace need to have all the fun. Might be nice to join in for once. And if anyone can bring that side out of me again, it'll be Mia.

Hell, this should be interesting at the very least.

'Okay thanks, man. I've gotta run.' I hang up wondering what the hell is going to happen next.

Mia *Fucking* Monroe.

Chapter Four

Mia

My eyes float over the room, taking it in. It's much larger than a hotel room—the ones I'm used to anyway. This guestroom is almost the size of my old apartment. Three large windows stretch up towards the vaulted ceilings. There's a walk in closet, a small oak desk and chair by one of the windows, and a seating area at the foot of the bed, with a loveseat covered in a purple floral pattern, and matching stuffed chair. I see why he calls it the purple room. It's subtle, but most of the furnishings have hints of purple. I wonder if he remembers that it's my favorite color. The thought makes me smile. But no, it would be silly for him to remember something so ridiculous, from so long ago.

The bed must be a king. I've never slept in anything so big. I wonder if I actually could, or if I'll spend the night getting lost in the expanse of it. At least it looks soft. So soft. The lavender duvet is as fluffy as a cloud, tempting me to run and jump into it. Instead, I head across the room and peek into the attached bath.

It's larger than any bathroom should be. There's a double sink, a Jacuzzi tub, and a separate large shower with more showerheads than I'd know what to do with. It's all so much that I feel my mouth actually fall open. If this is just a guest bedroom, what must the master bedroom be like?

Collins' family had always been well-off when we were growing up, but this is more than well-off, this is *wealthy*. I wonder if I had looked harder online, would I have found him on one of those richest men alive lists? It's intimidating. I feel like I've stumbled across a new culture and don't know the customs or the language. I tip toe across the room, careful not to disturb anything.

I had no idea he would be this affluent. Of course Collins was a born entrepreneur. When we were six and most kids were opening lemonade stands, he figured out that the markup value on ice cream treats, combined with his cute-kid factor would put him ahead of the game and setup a weekend neighborhood ice cream stand.

The local ice cream man didn't have a chance, and Collins made bank. Not that he needed it. No, I'm not surprised he is doing so well. I'm proud. He always had this in him. I smile at the thought.

I take another look around the room, and my eyes land on my huge suitcase. The one I packed with as many of my everyday things as I could, and a few very important items I didn't want to cram in my parent's small storage space.

Collins invited me to stay for a few days, so I might as well unpack. I hoist my suitcase up on the bed, unzip the front pouch, and pull out my old childhood scrapbook, flipping it open to the first page where I'd long ago glued the cover of a bridal magazine. The one Collins had found that fateful day hidden under my mattress.

I run my fingers over the crinkled paper, and smile as I remember the promise we'd made. It all started because of this very magazine. I'd found it at my babysitter's house, and loved it because it had a purple wedding dress on the cover. I never understood why brides always wore white and thought this elegant lavender gown was the very dress I would wear when I got married. I liked it so much that my babysitter let me take the magazine home. I'd been hiding it under my mattress, and Collins found it one day when we were playing in my room.

'Who's getting married?' he'd asked, wide eyed.

I snatched it away from him, trying to hide it a little too late. We might have been best friends, but he was still going through his *all girls have cooties* phase. Something I was normally immune from, but still, there were certain things I kept to myself. Or tried to. 'I am,' I proclaimed in the strongest voice I could. Still, I felt myself blush.

Collins wrinkled his nose and furrowed his brow in that way that made a small crinkle over one eyebrow. 'No way.'

I rolled my eyes. 'Not today. But one day.'

'I'll never get married. That's gross.' His eyes widened.

'Yes you will. Everyone does.'

'Okay, fine. But if I have to marry someone, I'm gonna marry you.' He poked me in the arm with his finger hard enough that it hurt, just a little.

It wasn't a romantic candle lit dinner with champagne and get down on one knee type of proposal, but at the age of ten, it was all I needed. And I wouldn't trade that memory for anything.

In my bedroom that day, we deliberated and it evolved into a promise that if neither of us had married by the time we were thirty, we'd married each other.

Pinky swear.

I'd turned thirty a few months ago, and the promise had been lurking in the back of my mind ever since. But did that mean I actually needed to spend the last few dollars I had running across country to see Collins? It seemed like a good idea at the time, but the more I analyze it now, the sillier the whole thing seems.

I pull out my phone and dial my friend Leila's number.

'Are you really there? I mean actually in LA,' she says by way of greeting.

'Yes,' I say.

'I can't believe you went, girl. You are crazy,' she shrieks in her usual over excited tone.

'You're the one who said I should go,' I say.

'So? We were drinking. Besides, I was 100% kidding and you know that.' I think back to when we met for drinks just after I was fired. We were talking over my options, or lack of options. I was about to get evicted for non-payment of rent. She offered me her sofa in the tiny one bedroom she shared with her husband and newborn. No thank you. Then suggested my parents' place, which was even smaller than hers. The next thing out of her mouth was a joke, 'Maybe you should move to LA and marry that Collins guy.'

She laughed. But I didn't. The mention of my childhood love made my cheeks warm and my belly churn. It seemed like an option, one as good as any other. Maybe even better. Just the thought of seeing Collins again had been so enticing.

But now that I was really here, I was questioning myself. 'I know,' I say. 'I shouldn't have come. He's got a live-in girlfriend, and she's super beautiful.'

'Mia, I'm sorry. But what did you expect?'

My inner romantic knows exactly what I expected. He was going to open the door, recognize me at once, and we would be married the next day. 'I know. It was childish of me to come.'

'But you're in his house? Does that mean he invited you to stay?'

'For a few days.'

'And he has a guest bedroom, or a couch or whatever?'

I laugh. 'It's more like a guest suite. He's doing really well. His house is amazing, Leila. He's got so many guest rooms they name them. I'm in the Purple Room.'

'Well, sounds like you might be okay there for a few days then. But remember—my couch is always open if you need a place to crash. And if things get weird there, I will find a way to loan you the money for a ticket home.'

I know she means it. Leila's a great friend, but there's no way I'll let them cut into their small savings to fly me home. Not with their newborn and all. 'No you won't. I'll be fine,' I say.

'The offer is there.'

'Thank you.'

We get off the phone, and I chew on my lip as I mull over my situation. When I told Collins what I was doing here, he seemed kind of stunned. Not that we ever really talked about it since we were interrupted by Tatianna's arrival.

There's a knock at the door. 'Mia, are you hungry?' Collins says through the door.

I pull it open. He and Tatianna are there.

'Sure.' And I absolutely am. The four-hour time difference means my stomach wants dinner *yesterday*.

'Dinner's ready. I asked the cook to set an extra plate for you.' He waves for me to follow them and I do. Collins and Tatianna walk next to each other, but manage to avoid physical contact and don't say a word as we make our way down to the dining room. I wonder if this is how they normally are together, or if I've caused this icy tension. The Collins I knew loved to talk. Some days we'd spend the entire day taking turns telling stories. Sure there were times we'd been quiet, but usually it was because we were reading, or watching something, or even just tired.

The silence between him and Tatianna seems different somehow. Not awkward exactly, but not comfortable either. It's like they don't have anything to say to each other, so they've just stopped talking. But surely there's always something to talk about. In all the years Collins and I were friends, I don't ever remember either one of us ever lacking in interesting things to say.

Collins stops at a doorway and motions for me to enter. Having adjusted my expectations to assume everything is huge in this house, I am not disappointed by the size of the dining room. I follow Tatianna down to the far end of what might more aptly be called a dining hall.

'Take a seat.' Collins points at one of the places made up at the end of a table long enough to seat twenty. I sit down and try not to gawk too much as I take in the two amazing crystal chandeliers that hang from above, elegantly illuminating the room. Collins takes the seat next to me, at the head of the table, and Tatianna seats herself on the other side of him and across from me. She barely takes her eyes off her phone as she pours herself some water.

I turn to Collins, wondering if this is the way she usually is when they eat dinner, but he doesn't seem to notice. I can't help thinking that if I were dating someone as amazing as Collins, I wouldn't be staring at my phone when he was around, I'd be gazing into his eyes.

The food is already served and on the table. Collins picks up a bottle of wine and fills my glass before filling his own. He doesn't offer any to Tatianna. In fact, she doesn't even have a wine glass.

Dinner is a baked chicken breast with grilled vegetables. Collins looks at it for a moment as if he's psyching himself up for it, and then picks up his silverware and starts cutting the chicken into pieces.

'When did you start liking poultry?' I ask as I cut into my own. I'll eat almost anything, but Collins had always been a bit of a picky eater, and disliked pretty much all fowl. He's more a red meat kind of guy. As I take my first bite, I notice Tatianna looking at him coolly, but not saying anything. Crap. Maybe I offended her. 'Not that I don't love it, I just meant...I guess we change with age, right?'

Collins finishes chewing, and chases his bite down with wine, then says, 'Tatianna doesn't eat red meat, so we don't really keep it in the house.' He looks as if he's talking sadly about a battle he's lost.

I guess it makes sense if they live together, they must eat a lot of their meals together. But as I glance at her plate I notice she's not even eating the same thing. Her plate is smaller, and piled with baby spinach and a small cherry tomato that's been quartered and spread around the edge to give it color. I have to hide my shock. If she's not even eating it, why should she care? It angers me that she would force her food preferences on him. Especially if they don't even eat the same thing. Why does she feel the need to change him? He was perfect to start with.

Collins eyes her plate, then looks up at her meaningfully, but doesn't say anything.

I wonder if he's realizing how stupid it is, too. I stab a piece of chicken a bit harder than I need to with my fork, and take a bite. Chewing it, I mentally talk myself out of glaring at her throughout dinner. This is her house too after all.

I take a deep breath and ask Collins more about his business as we eat. It's a bit weird. I was always the numbers girl, and yet, here he is, the owner of an investment firm. Being a bit of a numbers geek, I prod him all evening with questions about the inner workings of it all.

'Collins,' Tatianna jumps in while he takes a bite. 'As fascinating as this is, I'm about finished, and I have to call my agent. You don't mind if I leave you two, do you?' At this point, I realize she's tuned out virtually the entire conversation. If her phone hadn't been there to distract her, I wonder if she might rather count the individual pieces of spinach in her salad than talk about his work.

'No, go ahead,' he says. He kisses her cheek as she kisses the air next to his. I look at his hard square jaw, and smooth tan skin. How could she not want to brush her lips against that jawline?

'Nice meeting you, Mia,' she says glancing at me briefly before turning back to her phone and wandering off. She probably figures this is the last time she's going to see me, and hell, maybe it is.

Collins has a good life, a serious girlfriend, I can't just come barging in.

By dessert, I have a pretty good snapshot of how the money flows through an investment firm. Collins geeks out almost as much as me, and we lean over our chocolate lava cake as we talk about the inner-workings of his company. His eyes are vibrant as he talks about his business, and I can tell he really does love his work. The life in his eyes is something I haven't seen in a long time, and it fills me with warm energy.

When dinner is over, he walks me back up to my room, leaving me at the door.

'I've got some business to attend to before bed, but we'll be going out on the yacht tomorrow. I hope you'll join us. I think you'd love it.'

Just the idea of being on a boat with him brings images of that night back to me. I wonder if he's thinking about it again, too.

He looks down at me. We stand a foot apart, but there's a desire in his eyes to move closer. To be alone with him on his yacht sounds delicious. I think of his perfectly built adult body taking command and riding me and feel a throb between my legs.

I swallow, and remind myself that he invited me to go with him and his *girlfriend*. 'That would be fun,' I say.

He smiles and his eyes flit down my body briefly, making my cheeks flush. He didn't look at Tatianna that way. In fact, during dinner they'd hardly exchanged a look, let alone talked to each other. I have to wonder if he's happy with her. I mean he must be, they live together. But this evening at dinner, he didn't seem happy, at least not with her.

'Night,' he says.

'See you tomorrow.'

I close the door and my head is spinning. My pulse racing just from the thrill of being near him. I fall back on the bed and stare at the ceiling. He may not seem overly excited about the promise we made each other when we were ten, but he does seem genuinely happy to see me. It won't hurt if I stay a few days. I roll over and dig in my bag—which is still on the mammoth bed—and pull out my laptop, opening it up.

Maybe I can look for a job here. If he's really with Tatianna, I can't expect him to put me up forever. I need an exit strategy.

Just in case.

Chapter Five

Collins

I park my car in the marina lot and lead the way toward the docks. Tatianna's eyes are downcast on her phone, while Mia's are wide and her neck is craning to take in every ounce of her surroundings.

'Oh wow, this is…' She chews on her lip, searching for the word.

I know this is much different from how we grew up, but I don't want her to feel intimidated. 'I have a thing for boats.' I grin at her and wait for the double meaning in my comment to hit. Her cheeks flush pink and my dick throbs eagerly at the memory of her tight little body. I'm thankful for the cover of my aviator-style sunglasses. 'We'll have fun today,' I add, recovering.

'Yes.' She swallows and glances at Tatianna, who is following closely behind us, but absorbed in something on her phone as she so often is lately.

'This is her,' I say, pointing up ahead to where the sleek, white-hulled vessel rests in the water. She's big—but not obnoxiously so. Only seventy-feet, which is actually on the small side for a yacht. But she sleeps eight guests, in four private cabins, which is plenty big for my recreational use.

The staff has her all ready for us. The chrome fixtures have been polished and are sparkling in the sunlight, and I can see up on the main deck that the lounge chairs have been outfitted with pillows and towels. I offer Tatianna a hand and she climbs aboard. I glance back to see what's keeping Mia. She's still standing on the dock, her attention captured by something at the stern.

'Mia?' I climb down the steps and go to her.

She's staring at the purple cursive lettering I had painted at the stern, just above the swim platform.

'You named your boat Gremlin?' she asks with astonishment in her voice.

I shrug. 'It seemed fitting.' When I bought my boat, I could think of no better name than after my friend who I shared so many good times with—one of the most significant happening on a boat. Her eyes widen and find mine as the meaning behind the name sinks in.

'Come on.' I take her hand and lead her toward the stairs. 'I want to show you around.'

She squeezes my hand, and then follows me up on board.

Every inch of the yacht seems to amaze her, and I love the giddy excitement she openly displays. It's refreshing. She seems to like the theater room with its big screen and comfy reclining loveseats the best. 'The intent behind it is for rainy days, but we have so few of those in Southern California, that it's never been used. We mostly stay out on the deck,' I explain.

'I'm sure you and Tatianna come and stay the night here just for the fun of it, sometimes, right? Movie and popcorn night. That would be fun.'

My brow crinkles. 'No, actually we've never done that.'

Mia's confusion is written all over her face.

I decide to continue the tour. Showing her the bedrooms feels too intimate, especially given what happened between us the last time we were below deck together, so I merely point and continue walking.

Mia shuffles behind, her gaze bouncing around each room to absorb every detail.

No matter what is going on in my life, or at work, I always looked forward to Sundays. Fresh ocean air and blue skies are good for the soul.

I guide her back upstairs. The breeze is just beginning to pick up as we motor out of the harbor. The deck is outfitted with various couches and chairs arranged for conversation, there's a hot tub off to one side and then plenty of lounge chairs with fluffy cushions for sunbathing. That's where Tatianna has already stationed herself. As usual she's removed her top—her small pointy nipples are staring straight up at the sun. She sits up when she notices our arrival.

'Let me know if this makes you uncomfortable,' she says to Mia, gesturing to her naked chest. 'I don't like tan lines, but I can cover up if you prefer.'

Mia stares straight ahead, seemingly unfazed by Tatianna's display. 'I'm not uncomfortable.' Mia removes her own tank top from over her head, and I swear I see the whole thing in slow motion to the beat of hypnotic music. I am mesmerized. Mia has nothing to be ashamed of. Her chest is on the large side and is barely contained by the cups of her purple bikini top. If she wanted to follow suit and take off her top, there is no way my erection would go unnoticed. I already feel my cock stirring in my shorts, and I have to distract myself with gathering drinks.

I look down at my dick and curse at him. 'Not today, fucker,' I say under my breath while arranging cups with ice.

'What was that?' Mia asks, coming over to join me.

'Nothing,' I bite out. 'What would you like to drink?'

'Do you have lemonade?'

'Sure do.'

Breasts are one of the few areas where Tatianna hasn't been blessed, however, that doesn't mean I'm free to gawk at Mia's glorious, round tits. But dear God, it's like Christmas. I can't seem to keep my eyes from straying over to her chest. The soft mounds are pushed together thanks to the straining fabric, and her cleavage is plentiful. I want to bury my face between them and treat them to wet kisses. Mia in a bathing suit is holy hell, hot. I'm used to Tatianna's model-thin body with her lack of curves, and visible rib cage. Mia has soft rounded flesh that I want to sink my teeth into. I can't stop staring, and I'm hoping the heated gazes I'm sending her aren't obvious.

'Collins?' Tatianna asks, pulling my attention away.

'Yeah?' My voice comes out tense and too rough. I clear my throat and try again.

'Can I have sparkling mineral water with a slice of cucumber?' she asks.

'Of course.' I head to the kitchen to retrieve a cucumber, thankful for the moment away from Mia. I have no idea why she's affecting me this way, but I know I need to get my head on straight.

We settle in for some sunbathing, but after an hour of sitting quietly in the sun, Mia declares herself officially bored and wanders off in search of something to entertain herself.

There are books and board games in a cabinet inside, and I expect her to return with one of those, but when she makes her way back on deck fifteen minutes later, she's carrying several foam noodles and one of the crew members—James, I think—is attaching a giant inflatable slide I didn't even know I had over the side of the boat.

'I hope you don't mind, but I asked the captain if we could stop to swim,' Mia says.

'Swim?' Tatianna and I both ask in unison. Tatianna sits up and watches as the slide is attached.

'Yeah, unless you're chicken,' Mia taunts, waving one of the noodles at me.

I rise and remove my sunglasses. 'I'm game.' I can only sit in the sun for so long. Typically after an hour or so, I head inside and check my email while Tatianna continues sunning herself to a deep bronzed glow.

'Are you seriously going to go down that thing?' Tatianna asks, eyeing the slide with disdain.

'Sure, why not?' I shrug.

'I'm not getting in that freezing cold water,' Tatianna says, laying down again. 'You two have fun.' She lifts the fashion magazine she was reading back in front of her face.

When I get close, Mia spanks me across the ass with a noodle. An unexpected laugh falls from my lips. There is something so playful and whimsical about her personality. She can still make me forget myself and just let go, despite our years apart. She's always possessed that skill. It was most helpful right after my mom passed away. I needed that levity more than ever, and Mia provided it. And I suppose now is no different. I like that she doesn't act her age.

'Come on. I'll let you go first down the slide,' she says.

'Let me, huh?' I lift one eyebrow. I pick her up and set her down on the top of the slide. It doesn't escape my notice that she's removed the shorts she'd been wearing all afternoon. Her bikini bottoms don't match the top. They're lime green. And the rounded curve of her ass cheeks peeking from the bottom is highly distracting. 'Down you go.' I place my hands on her shoulders and give her a playful push while still holding her securely.

'You wouldn't.' She glares at me while her mouth is curved up into a crooked grin.

'Maybe I'm not as nice as the guy you remember.'

'You're perfect,' she says, her face going serious for a moment.

She can't say things like that. It's confusing as shit. The conversation I had with Colton last night spins in my brain. He was convinced that I've been in love Mia since I was a kid.

'Collins?' she asks, her face still holding its serious expression.

'Plug your nose,' I tell her and give her a shove.

Mia goes barreling down the slide toward the ocean and just before I hear the splash, she lets out a playful squeal.

We take turns heaving ourselves down the inflatable slide—on our backs, bellies and sides. We hit the water with force and laughter, swimming—or in her case, dog-paddling—over to the ladder to climb back on board and repeat it again and again. It's like I've been transported back to a simpler time. I feel like I'm six years old again without a care in the world. We're both shivering and the salt-water stings our eyes, but our smiles refuse to fade. I've never had so much fun yachting. Tatianna glances up at us occasionally, but when I encourage her to join us, she turns over in her chair, saying she needs to sun her back.

'Last one in the water's a rotten egg!' Mia calls and hits the slide at a run—flinging herself down on her stomach. I hear a splash at the bottom and then nothing else. She usually comes up laughing. My stomach drops.

'Mia?' I peer over the side of the boat.

She's there, treading water, but with a worried expression. Shit. She probably hurt herself going over like that.

I grab a noodle and go barreling down the slide toward her. I hit the water and swim to the surface, pulling in a breath and immediately swimming hard toward her. She's facing away from me, a few feet away. 'Mia? What happened? Are you okay?'

'Don't come over here,' she warns.

What the hell? 'Mia?'

'I'm serious, Collins.'

She's not the strongest swimmer, and when I see her head dip under the water, I wrap her in my arms and pull her up, securing the noodle around her. 'Come here. I've got you.'

'You can't see me like this.'

I look down, trying to understand what she means. Fuck me. Her top is off. Gone. And dear God, her breasts are every bit as glorious as I imagined. Full and round with pink nipples just begging to be sucked. Hard.

'My top flew off when I hit the water. I tried looking for it, but I think it sank.'

Thank you, gravity.

'I've seen it all before, sweetheart,' I remind her.

She swallows and blinks at me, little droplets of water clinging to her dark eyelashes. 'Yes, but I've grown since then.'

'Trust me, I noticed.'

She punches me in the shoulder. 'Be serious.'

'I am one-hundred-fucking-percent serious right now.' She's still pulling away from me, still trying to cover her chest with one arm while she paddles with the other. 'Stop struggling, Mia. You'll only tire yourself out.'

She makes a small noise of defeat, then stops fighting long enough for me to pull her close.

I am wholly unprepared for the heat of her naked skin against mine, the hard peaks of her nipples rubbing against my bare chest. It sends instant awareness to my cock. The troublemaker has been looking for an opportunity to come out and play all day.

Having a mostly naked woman in my arms is no contest for the chill of the water, and warm tingles shoot through me, heating me quickly.

'There you go. I've got you.' My voice drops low.

She wraps her arms around my shoulders and I tread water, easily keeping us afloat with the help of the foam noodle.

'That's it. Just relax.'

'I'm sorry.'

'Shh, it's okay.'

Her gorgeous green eyes lift to mine and I can feel her heart thumping against my chest. The moment feels heavy with antici-pation. I have a half-naked Mia in my arms, and I can't help but remember the last time we were in this position. Part of me regrets it. She was too young; I was too rough with her. God, what I wouldn't give for a do-over. I've never wanted anything as bad. Shit, I don't know where that thought came from.

I hold her close and swim as best as I can toward the stern of the yacht and the ladder attached to the swim platform.

When we reach the platform, I grab hold of the ladder, but I'm in no hurry to have her disentangle herself from me, or climb back aboard. I tighten my grip around her waist. Mia remains hanging on to me, watching me curiously, waiting to see what I'll do.

'Are you okay?' I ask.

She nods. 'You rescued me. You've always rescued me,' she breathes, her mouth just inches from mine.

She brings her legs around my waist, and her core brushes against my erection, tearing a strangled groan from my throat. Her eyes widen in surprise.

'Don't move,' I growl.

Ignoring my request, she tightens her legs around me, her center rubbing against my cock with the most exquisitely frustrating friction I can imagine. A feeling of wild, uncontained desire roars through me. She makes a tiny sound of pleasure in the back of her throat.

Just as I lean in toward her, Mia's eyes fall closed. Our mouths meet in a rush of hungry kisses. She tastes of salt water and her lips are cold, but her tongue is greedy, taking every stroke I give her and matching it with seductive skill.

My hands itch to cup her gorgeous breasts, to tug on her sexy nipples and hear her moan, but I hold onto her, unwilling to let go. One hand grips the ladder to keep us afloat and my mouth stays fused to hers.

She rocks against me, the heat of her pussy owning me beneath the water. She lets out a little cry of pleasure when she feels how hard I am. For her. Only for her.

'Christ, Mia,' I groan, breaking my mouth away from hers. I feel like I'm going to explode.

From the moment I saw her, all I've thought about it getting my lips on hers. When she meets my eyes, I can tell we're both thinking the same thing. Even after all these years, we can both still feel it. The unexplored sexual tension burns hotly between us. The question is, what am I going to do about it?

Chapter Six

Mia

The kiss feels so right, so perfect. The water might be cold, but our bodies are on fire with heat from the friction as we press together. Collins' warm arms hold me close, and I push my chest and my core against him. My entire body is overheating, and I feel as though we are melting into one being.

It's that right.

When Collins somehow manages to pull away, it's as if he's ripping us in two.

I'm so flustered, and in such a haze that even with the harsh separation, I still gaze at him. His eyes match my lust and my need. I search his face looking for anything, any reason we can't be together. Because it feels so perfect, him and me. I can see it in his eyes, he feels it too. That zing between us, this temptation, this desire hasn't gone away over time. My racing heart and his gasping for breath suggest the heat between us, hasn't faded at all—it's grown.

Before, fifteen years ago, we were two curious friends. We cared for each other, sure. But here, today, there's something more. It's barely been twenty-four hours since I arrived here, and I feel so drawn to him, that I'm not sure how I can possibly back away.

Yet I know I have to. His face changes and his eyes dart up to the boat. He's remembering his girlfriend, who we've left on

40

deck. My stomach drops, and I think I might too. If he let me go right now, I might sink to the bottom of the ocean. Not because I wanted to die, but because without him, I wasn't sure if I had the energy to live.

'Are you happy with her?' I ask.

He still holds me, but he maneuvers me to the ladder. 'I…' he pauses and looks at me pleadingly. And then I can't read his face anymore. It's as if he's shut me out. 'I don't know.' He says it as if he truly isn't sure, but he's also not sure he's ready to end it with her.

I sigh and turn away, gripping the ladder. As he backs away, I feel the cold of the water surrounding me, and I shiver. Suddenly, I have an urgent need to get up the ladder and get warm. I pull myself up. My teeth chatter like mad. Even though Tatianna is around the corner and the crew is out of sight, I cover myself as best as I can and rush for the pile of new fluffy towels someone has left out for us.

Seriously, how many staff are aboard this thing? I wonder.

'Mia?' Collins has followed me up.

He heads toward me. Water drips from his tan, muscular torso. A scene I'd been enjoying for the last hour and still know I will never tire of. His body is so firm. His skin is soft yet hot to the touch. I might as well just rip off my bikini bottoms and hand them over to him. It is nearly impossible to turn away. But I do and rush to throw on my tank. I'm humiliated. If he's really staying with her, he doesn't get any more free shows. Nope.

'I'm sorry, Mia,' he says. He places his strong hand gently on my shoulder and guides me around to face him.

I'm forced to look again into his amazing blue eyes and wait for him to say more.

He rubs his hand over his wet hair and says. 'My life is complicated. It's not as easy as it was when we were little. We can't just pinky swear and then live happily ever after.'

His words hurt so much I flinch. I can't tell if I believe them, but they must be right. Because I hear them all the time. My parents always tell me I'm a dreamer. Leila says I'm too romantic. I've always taken the comments as playful jabs. But hearing it from him, for some reason that hurts. Maybe it's time I finally accept it. I wipe away a tear and take in a shaky breath, nodding. 'Yeah. I know. It's not a fairytale; it's real life. You two have been together for a long time.' I step back and wave him off, blotting my eyes with my towel.

'Lunch,' Tatianna shouts from around the corner.

Collins eyes lock on mine. 'Sorry,' he mouths.

I want to tell him it's okay, that I'll be all right. But I can't find the words, because it feels like someone just punched me in the stomach.

So instead, I just nod and follow him around to the bow where a table has been set for our lunch. Thankfully, Collins pulls his shirt back on before he sits down. My ego is hurt, and still I'm going to have a hard enough time keeping my eyes from visually molesting him—even without him being half naked.

'My agent set up a few shoots for me this week. We don't have anything going on, right?' Tatianna asks Collins.

He glances at me before answering her. 'Uh, no. We're clear.'

'I figured it was fine,' she smiles at me then at Collins. 'I mean you two have all your catching up to do or whatever. It's not like you guys want me around for that. You can spend some time together. You know, show Mia a good time.'

My face flushes, and I look down at my sandwich. She has no idea how close her words bring me to a nervous laughing fit. She also, apparently, has no idea what just happened between Collins and me. Her face shows not a hint of being jealous or worried that I might pose a threat to her relationship with Collins. And now that I look at her, with her perfect hair and beautiful face—not to mention her beyond elegant body—I have no idea why someone who was dating her would want to kiss me, let alone dump her for me.

Maybe Collins is right. I'm living in a fairytale, and it is time to grow up.

Besides, Collins and I had been best friends before, there is no reason we can't continue that now. I'd applied for several jobs last night online. If I can land one, I'll be able to move out of his house, soon, and we can totally do the *friend* thing.

I think.

Having cleared her schedule with Collins, Tatianna tunes out once more, getting lost in her phone as she nibbles on her plate of lettuce. Leaving Collins and me to silently look at one another. Leaving me to wonder why I'd been so bold as to kiss this woman's boyfriend. I'm not that type of person. I don't go after guys who are already taken, but then there is no other guy like Collins Drake. And I'd claimed him years ago.

Laying guilt on top of the humiliation I already feel, I'm surprised I can eat at all, but when I take a bite of my sandwich, I discover how hungry the morning's activities have made me. It's not bad at all for chicken salad. In fact, I manage to inhale it. Something Collins appears to enjoy watching.

Being ravenous and distracted is a poor combination, and I manage to bite my tongue. 'Ouch,' I say.

Collins bursts out laughing. 'Slow down, Mia. We wouldn't want you to choke on your tongue.'

I give him a snarky smirk. But I notice that Collins isn't eating. Darn Tatianna and her chicken fetish.

He sips his beer, quietly, and I forget about Tatianna.

I can't help watching his lips on the beer bottle. It reminds me of how smooth his lips were as they brushed against mine, and how commanding his kiss was. His mouth was so demanding, and

I loved the way he held me firmly as he took what he wanted from me. And he had *wanted* me at that moment, in the water. I felt it, rock hard and even bigger, so much bigger than I remembered. I get wet just thinking of how big he was, pushed up against me. At the moment I realized how hard he was for me, I wanted to slip my hand inside his swimsuit and feel him in my hands. The only thing stopping me was the fear of letting go of my iron grip around him. The only thing that was saving me from falling into the depths of the Pacific.

Collins choses that exact moment to look up and meet my eyes. His look smolders as his gaze drops from my eyes to my mouth. He's thinking about the kiss too.

'I had fun with you in the water, Mia,' Collins says pulling me back into the present. His voice is slow and sensuous. 'I haven't done anything like that in a long time.' His eyes sparkle, and he smiles unevenly. My stomach flips as my body reacts to his words.

I lean forward on my elbows and the desire for him, for all of this, rears its head. His eyes flash on mine, and for a second, he's wondering if I'm going to out him, and our water activities. 'I don't know how you could spend every Sunday out here and not go swimming,' I say, sweetly.

His eyes soften and I can tell he's relieved. It feels so good to see him happy.

After lunch, Collins tells me to make myself at home before he takes his leave to go get a bit of work done.

I barely consider tanning with Tatianna. I don't want to be the other woman, but I don't really want to be her bestie either. Besides, I'm tired. I didn't sleep well last night, strange bed and all, and since he told me to make myself at home, I will find a nice place to take a nap.

I go inside in search of one of the many bedrooms.

He described this as a smaller yacht, but to me it's huge. I turn a corner expecting to find the bedrooms, but walk right into the kitchen where I find several of the staff sitting around making their own sandwiches for lunch. I'm about to apologize and turn around when I notice that they have roast beef.

'Excuse me,' I say, eyeing the roast beef. 'Would you guys mind if I made myself a sandwich?'

They shrug and nod, so I step in further and help myself to bread, open the fridge to see what sort of fixings they have.

When I finish making the sandwich I halve it and put it on a plate, and head out up to the indoor seating area where I know Collins is working. I find him at his computer, deeply engaged, so much so that I'm able to set the sandwich next to him and rush out just as he looks up to see it.

'Hey,' he hollers at me.

I turn at the door. 'Sorry. I couldn't stand the thought of you working on an empty stomach.'

He meets my eyes with a meaningful look. 'Thank you.' I don't know if he's thanking me for that kiss, or for not saying anything to Tatianna, or for the sandwich.

'You're welcome.'

I watch with satisfaction as he takes a huge bite. 'You know what I like.' I'm pretty sure he's talking about the sandwich at the moment, but I can't help blushing.

I nod and smile. Then head back down to find a nice place for a nap.

Chapter Seven

Collins

I'm sitting up in bed with my laptop perched beside me, when Tatianna crawls into my lap.

'I'm going to be gone for the next few nights,' she whispers, bringing her mouth to my neck.

'Where's the shoot this time?' I ask, peering around her head to finish typing the email I'm trying to send.

'In Utah,' she says. 'I'm modeling a fall line for Calvin Klein.'

I always find it interesting how they plan a season ahead. She does swimwear work in the dead of winter for the following spring, and in the summertime, she models winter coats.

'Do you want me to take you to the airport on my way to work in the morning?' I ask.

She chuckles. 'No. That's not why I brought up my trip. I'm going to be gone for the next couple of nights.' She wiggles her eyebrows at me. 'I want some.' Her hand reaches lower and she grabs onto my package, giving him a gentle squeeze. I'm soft, but she doesn't seem to care.

She brings her lips to mine, and I kiss them, dutifully, but something about it feels off.

'Not tonight,' I tell her. There is no way I'd feel right being intimate with Tatianna knowing that Mia is right down the hall. 'I'm tired, and I have a few more things to finish yet.'

'Why are you so stressed out, babe?' she asks, pressing her fingers to my temples and lightly rubbing.

'Mm, that feels nice.' I close my eyes and enjoy the relaxing sensation. She continues lightly rubbing, moving her hands into my hair and massaging my scalp.

I feel Tatianna's lips against mine again and her pelvis press into me. 'Come on, Collins, I want to have sex,' she breathes against my mouth. Her lips are stiff and practiced. I don't know why I would just now notice that after three years of dating her.

I can't help but recall the feeling of hot Mia's mouth against mine. Her lips were full and lush and moved so easily with mine. I remember her suntanned curves, the freckles across the bridge of her nose, and the water droplets clinging to her dark eyelashes just before I took her mouth. Her tongue was shy at first, but when I deepened the kiss, she licked against my tongue and then sucked it into her mouth with a soft tug. My cock hardens at the memory.

'That's it, babe,' Tatianna says encouraging, rubbing herself against my erection.

Fuck. I'm hard, but it's not for Tatianna.

I remove her from my lap and rise from the bed. 'I'm not feeling well tonight.' Why am I lying to her?

'What's going on, Collins?' Her eyes narrow on mine and they're full of confusion. I know she's remembering the last time we had sex I couldn't even orgasm. For which I still have no answer, because Mia wasn't even here at that point.

Mia.

A fresh wave of memories flood my brain. The way her tight nipples felt against my chest, the way her generous ass felt in my palms as I held her in the water…

I adjust my erection and head into the bathroom, locking the door behind me.

Placing both palms flat against the travertine counter, I stare straight ahead into the mirror. *What in the fuck is going on with me?* Dark blue eyes stare back at me, looking lost and uncertain. Everything in my life is so exact and calculating, I'm at a loss about what's happening to me. Am I sick? Dying? I take several deep breaths and force myself to relax. I pace the large bathroom, walking from one end to the other while I try to clear my head.

Earlier, out in the cold water, when I'd kissed Mia's soft lips, the promise we'd made to each other came rushing back. We haven't talked seriously about that childhood promise, but shit, maybe we need to. There is obviously unsettled business between us, but the idea of marriage is insane. We were ten years old for fuck's sake. You can't decide who you're going to spend the rest of your life with in fifth grade. I don't even know if I want to get married. I haven't ever given the concept much thought. Maybe it's time I do, that way I can explain to Mia why it was a silly childhood fantasy, and why it can never happen. She will have to see reason.

I sink down onto the edge of the marble tub and push my hands into my hair. Christ, when did my life get so complicated? I have a woman who I've lived with for three years now, who I share my bed with, who fits into my carefully crafted plans. Then I have a woman who knows me, the *real* me, behind all the CEO corporate bullshit. She has completely upheaved my life in the space of 48 hours. She's warm and giving, and I feel lighter in her presence. She's fun and easy-going, nothing like Tatianna. Maybe her being here will prove to be a good thing. Get me to lighten up a little.

When I reenter the bedroom, Tatianna is curled onto her side, sound asleep. I pull back the blankets on my side of the bed and crawl in beside her. I should wake her and apologize, but instead, I let her sleep and grab my phone from the bedside table.

Before I even have time to process what I'm doing, I text Mia.
I had fun with you today.
Me too.

Her reply is almost instant. It makes me wonder if she's lying in bed just down the hall thinking of me, a thought that makes me happy.

I'm contemplating what to write next when another text from her comes through.
Why are you texting me when you're in bed with a supermodel?
Maybe being in bed with a supermodel isn't all it's cracked up to be.
You shouldn't talk that way about your GIRLFRIEND.

It doesn't escape my notice that the word girlfriend is in all caps.
I know. I'm sorry, I'm being a dick.

She doesn't reply. I wait several minutes, wondering what's going on inside her head. I wonder if she's thinks I'm a piece of shit for kissing her today when I'm with someone else.

I wonder how long this is going to last—me and Tatianna. I can already feel myself pulling away from her. The only thing that scares me about ending things with Tatianna is the realization that then I'd have to face my future with Mia. Am I ready for that? Do I want a future with Mia?

Finally, I decide to text Mia again.
Do you forgive me?
I do… But Collins, about that marriage promise we made…

My stomach sinks. I tap out a hasty reply.
Let's not talk about that yet.
Okay.

Chapter Eight

Mia

Sunday's yacht outing was confusing to say the least.

He named his boat *Gremlin*. A name he used to call me with so much affection. Then, he kissed me in the water. And he was so eager, so hungry for it. He'd held me so close. And he was so hard. Just remembering the heat and his growl as I pressed my core against him makes me clench my sex. I can't help but think how good it would feel to have the length of him fill me.

But then he pushed me away. He wants to stay with Tatianna. If I know anything about Collins, it's that he gets whatever he wants. There is no use trying to sway him. He chose her, and it's time for me to find peace with that and move on.

Crap.

The following morning, Tatianna catches her flight and Collins heads into work, leaving me alone in the huge house.

I spend the next couple of days applying for more jobs. Tightening up my resume, making spreadsheets of job openings, and systematically searching out the best opportunities. I know the economy is still weak, but I have unlimited free time to look for a job, and I can't stand the thought of living off Collins forever. It's either fly home in defeat, or actually try to make a go of this fresh start I so desperately need.

I've applied for ten jobs, and have leads on another ten. I've also driven myself nuts hitting the refresh button on my email in the hopes that I will have a job offer, or at least an interview. But that afternoon brings some relief. Collins must feel bad for leaving me alone at his house because he sends his brothers' significant others, Sophie and Kylie, over to take me out and show me around. Normally I would be weary of being setup on a blind *playdate*, but I am desperate to get out of the house.

I am more than a little anxious about meeting Sophie and Kylie. No matter how many times I tell myself I'm moving on and have no chance with Collins, it still feels like I'm about to meet 'the family,' and I find myself wanting them to like me in the worst way.

I've heard enough about how well off Colton and Pace are, and I'm terrified they've hooked up with the stereotypical high-society women—the kind that stare down their nose at you. On the other side, I'm also a little worried that they might be more boring than Tatianna.

My fears about them are dashed immediately. Although Sophie is young, she's an absolute charm and a half. Kylie is closer to my age, and I envy her for what a strong woman she is and instantly hope we will be good friends.

We go to a bar where, even though I know I can't afford it, I down my first cocktail in an effort to calm my nerves. I'm about to order a second when I see the prices on their drink menu. I try to hide my shock as I discreetly pull open my wallet and count how much I have left.

'Don't worry, this afternoon is on Collins,' Kylie says. 'We were instructed to not let you pay for anything.' She smiles at me.

'I insist,' I say, because even though it's more than I can afford, I don't want to be a burden to Collins.

Sophie laughs and waves me off. 'We aren't really used to all the money they throw around, either. Neither of us came from money.

Colton always tells me I don't need to worry about money; I don't need to ask before I buy things. But it still feels weird, you know?'

I nod. I don't know exactly, since I have hardly any money myself, but I get what she means. 'The wealth around these guys is insane,' I say. 'I always knew Collins was smart, and driven, but it's still really crazy to see how well they've done for themselves.'

'What brings you to LA?' Kylie asks.

'I lost my job,' I say. Telling them about the marriage promise seems too private. I like them, but I've only just met them. I take a sip of my cocktail, hoping it will give me the strength to tell this story again. There's no good spin for getting fired. Even if it wasn't my fault, it's still humiliating. 'I found myself with no money and nowhere to go. So I guess you could say I came here for a fresh start.'

Kylie's brow furrows. Oh dear, I can tell I've said something she doesn't like. Fear rushes through me.

She shakes her head. 'So, what? You saw your old buddy, Collins, on the list of the wealthiest Americans, and decide to come here and live off him?'

Nervous laughter makes vodka lemonade nearly shoot out my nose. *Shit, that burns.* My eyes tear from the sting. 'Oh my god, no. It's all a bit more embarrassing, and...' I shrink and blush, '...maybe a bit crazier than that.' I take another fortifying sip of my drink.

Sophie and Kylie share a questioning look, then lean in and wait for me to explain.

I'm mortified at the thought of telling these two why I am really here. Seriously, I'm such a romantic dork. Why am I here? Oh, because my best friend and I made a promise to each other that if we were both single when we turned thirty, we'd marry each other... Yeah, that sounds too crazy. Why the heck had I come? Because when I hit rock bottom, I wanted to be with the one person who made me feel like I was worth something.

By the way they look at me, I can tell they'll never trust or accept me if I don't tell them the sad truth.

I take a deep breath and tell them my story. The one about a ten-year-old girl who was head over heels in love with her best friend, Collins. I tell them about the moment in my room when he jabbed me in the arm with his finger and said he wanted to marry me. I stare at my hands the whole time and feel my palms sweat as I tell the story I haven't told anyone in such a long time.

When I finish, I look up and their eyes are softer and their smiles lighter. I can see right away that telling them was the right thing. And it's relieving to tell them. I'm desperate to hear their reactions.

'Awe,' Sophie sighs. 'That's right, you've known the guys forever. What were they like?'

Kylie folds her arms in front of her and leans in more. 'Yeah, what were the boys like growing up?'

I think back. For me it was always all about Collins, but I know they're asking about Colton and Pace. 'They've always been obnoxious together. Three brothers growing up in one house, there's bound to be a lot of rowdiness. Some days I'd come over to play with Collins and, the house would be shaking from the roughhousing. It was definitely something to experience.' I smile thinking back to one time in particular. 'Once Colton and Pace were wrestling, and they almost tumbled right into me. Collins saw it as it happened, and rushed over and threw himself between me and the rough and tumble mass of his younger brothers. My hero.' I blush as I realize I've said the last part out loud. But their smiles haven't faded and their curious looks beg me to tell more.

'Sometimes, when they weren't roughhousing,' I continue, 'they did this thing they called a laugh-off, trying to tell the best jokes, make the best funny faces. Whatever they could do to make each other laugh so hard they couldn't breathe.'

Sophie holds out her hand. 'Wait, you mean Colton and Pace right? Collins would never goof off like that.'

'What do you mean?' I give Sophie a sideways glance. 'He was usually the instigator. When Pace and Colton were small, Collins loved to chase them around making silly faces with threats of tickling. He was out of control.' As I say this, I think of the Collins I knew when I was younger. He loved to pretend like he was serious, but when his silly side came out, that was when he truly shined. Sometimes he would make me laugh so hard I'd almost pee.

I try to imagine Collins doing that now. It's harder to see, although when we were playing on the boat yesterday, that sparkle had been there in his eyes. For a while he'd laughed out loud, fully enjoying himself like I recall from all my best memories.

Sophie smiles and looks around, like she's got a secret. 'Mia, I don't know that I was supposed to share this with you, but Colton says Collins is in love with you.'

My face must show the shock I feel from her words because she adds, 'He says it like a joke, but I can tell there's some truth to what he's saying.' She winks.

Kylie waves her hand and chimes in, 'You are so much better for him than Tatianna. I mean, she's nice, but you actually care about him.' She crosses her arms and leans back. 'I can see it in your eyes when you talk about him.'

I try super hard not to internalize what they've just said, but it's nearly impossible. That he could possibly feel the same way I feel about him, and has all these years, would be so wonderful. But I know this is just the romantic in me grasping at whatever thread I can, to hold onto my happily ever after—my fairytale ending.

As the sun begins its descent towards the ocean, Kylie announces that it's time for them to drop me off. She's got to get home.

And it hits me. I don't have a home. As she drives me back to Collins' house, I begin to wonder what the heck I'm still doing here. Collins made his decision. He's staying with Tatianna. I shouldn't stay. I could move back home and live on Leila's couch while I look for a job.

But that doesn't sound any better than what I'm doing here. And at least here my reputation hasn't been sullied by lies. I have a shot at finding a new job. It wouldn't hurt to at least give the city a chance.

Besides, I'm not even sure he wants to be with Tatianna. I see how they are together. I see how cold she is. And he's not fawning all over her either. The other night he'd texted me while he was in bed with her. With *her*.

Why would he text me when his girlfriend is there and about to leave town for several days?

I still have the last text he sent me that night. His reaction to my mention of our childhood promise.

Let's not talk about that yet.

Yet? When I texted him, I was planning to let him off the hook. But he seems to think there's something still worth talking about. And that sticks with me. In fact, it's driving me nuts.

As Kylie pulls into Collins' long drive, I determine that I will confront him about it. I hate the idea of thrusting myself between Collins and his girlfriend, but I can't continue living in his house in this state of limbo. I'm not sure what he wants exactly, but I don't think he wants Tatianna. I'm not sure if he wants me. But I need to know.

Chapter Nine

Collins

With Tatianna out of town, there is no way I can go home. A whole house alone with Mia? *Fuck no.* That would only lead to trouble, and I'm not ready to put myself in a situation like that. At least I'm smart enough to know better. When I picture her big green eyes that follow me around the room, her soft curves that beg for my hands, and the way she always seems so concerned about how I'm doing, if I've had enough to eat... I don't know how to handle her. For once in my life, I'm at a loss about what to do.

So after work, I head over to Colton's place where he and Pace are enjoying a drink in the library. Colton recently added a billiard table and a bar, effectively renovating it into his own personal man-cave.

'There's the old man,' Pace greets me with a smile.

He and Colton have both been teasing me ever since I turned thirty. Pace had the balls to check my hair for grays the last time we had drinks. *The fucker.*

'What's up, boys?' I ask, sinking down into a leather armchair.

'You tell us,' Colton says, handing me a glass of scotch. 'Mia still roomies with you and Tatianna?'

He makes it sound like some sordid arrangement, but shit, maybe it is. My thoughts about her aren't exactly innocent. No, more like dark fantasies that involve her naked skin slapping up against mine.

I clear my throat and mumble 'It's fine.' But my answer must be too quick, because it sets off Colton's bullshit meter.

Colton laughs. 'You are so full of shit. When are you going to wake up and realize that you and Tatianna have nothing in common, other than great sex, and the girl you've been in love with your entire life is right under your nose?'

I focus on my drink. I won't tell Colt that the sex isn't so great – in fact I can't even get off. 'Pace, what's new with you?' I ask.

Colton curses under his breath, while Pace laughs at my obvious attempt at a topic change.

'I'm trying to get Kylie pregnant,' he announces, proudly.

'No shit?' Colton and I ask in unison.

'You guys aren't even married yet,' I point out.

He shrugs. 'Close enough. We're engaged.'

I smile because I hated to see the way Pace always used to flounder with women. As a guy I always understood it, but as the oldest brother, I had to worry about him. When he found Kylie, watching him make the change from perpetual womanizer to family man was a relief. 'Well, you shouldn't have too much of a challenge getting her knocked up. Lord knows you've had enough practice.'

'You're not getting off that easily, brother,' Colton says, turning toward me. The douche is going to make me talk about Mia.

I try to take another sip of my drink and realize I've downed the entire glass. *Shit.*

Colton smirks at me and holds up the decanter of scotch. 'You want some more of this?'

I narrow my eyes.

'Then you're going to have to actually talk to us. Like a grown up. No more of this grunting and evading caveman bullshit. Tell us what's going on,' Colton says.

'Give me the damn scotch,' I bark.

He hands it over and I pour myself a healthy measure while deciding exactly what I'm going to tell them.

Pace leans back in his seat, crossing his feet at his ankles, and Colton settles in, getting comfortable too. Here we go, it's fucking sharing time, apparently.

'When Mia and I were kids, we sort of promised each other that if neither of us was married by the time we were thirty, we'd marry each other.'

Colton chokes on his liquor, coughing and sputtering loudly. 'You've got to be kidding me.'

Pace chuckles to himself. 'That's fucking brilliant. You should totally do that.'

Neither of their responses is encouraging.

I expect them to tease the shit out of me for entertaining Mia's childhood promise, which they do, but then the conversation shifts and I find them debating the actual merits of this marriage promise while I down glass after glass of scotch. Finally, Colton takes the bottle away and places it across the room.

'Shit, man,' Colton says. 'You don't have to march down the aisle with her tomorrow or anything, but I know you. You get this possessive-ass 'mine' caveman look whenever you talk about Mia. Something you never do when you talk about Tatianna.'

I feel fuzzy and unsure. And the longer I sit here, the more uncertain I become. A childhood marriage proposal is crazy right? That's just some stupid thing kids say—it doesn't mean anything. Does it? Mia seems to believe it does. She'd shown up here, just months after her birthday. My heart pounds faster when I think about that fact.

Colton asks about Tatianna again, and that's just not a topic I'm ready to discuss.

'I honestly don't see why you're still with her, bro,' Pace says.

'Seriously man, if she doesn't make you happy—break up with her,' Colton adds.

I lift my glass to my lips, like more liquor will help me figure out what to do. Leaning back in my chair, I close my eyes and let the alcohol warm me. I allow myself to picture what my life would be like with Mia in it. Dangerous to be sure. I see kids running around with her auburn hair and green eyes, Sundays on the yacht, my home filled with laughter and love. I'm warmed by the idea. Or maybe that warm tingly sensation is the alcohol. Either way, I think it's time to go home.

Pace gives me a ride and drops me off at my front door. The house is dark and quiet with Tatianna gone and Mia likely in bed by now. I head to my bedroom and get a text on my phone.

It's Mia.

Are you home?

Yes.

Where were you?

Brothers.

I don't know what else to say, because it's strange knowing that I spent the whole evening talking with them about the two women in my life and still don't know where I stand.

Sounds like fun.

I was trying to figure out some shit with my life.

We don't have to text, she's not here. Meet you in the kitchen? We can eat the peanut butter directly from the jar like old times and talk about it.

My heart slams against my ribs. Tatianna's not home, as Mia pointed out. And the idea of seeing Mia right now fills me with longing. But I'm drunk. And even through the alcohol haze, I know it's a piss poor idea.

I don't trust myself.

With the peanut butter?

59

With you.
Her reply takes several minutes to come through.
Oh.
We need to talk tomorrow when I'm sober.
Okay.

When I wake in the morning, it feels like a dead rat crawled down my throat and set up shop. I blink against the harsh light and curse at myself for drinking so much last night. I vaguely recall Pace dropping me off at home, and then texting with Mia.

Mia.

I told her we would talk about things today.

With a deep sigh, I force myself out of bed, shower and dress. It's Saturday, which means I should be going to kickboxing, but with the amount of alcohol I consumed last night, that's not happening.

I make my way downstairs, in desperate need of coffee, and find Tatianna in the kitchen. 'Oh, you're back.' With everything on my mind lately, I'd forgotten she texted me about her change in travel plans.

She lifts up on her toes and kisses my cheek. 'I told you I'd be back today.'

While I start the coffee, she fills me in on her trip. Apparently, the photographer was difficult to work with. No surprise there. Tatianna finds most people difficult to work with.

Twisting the cap off a bottle of water, Tatianna turns to me. 'So what did you and Mia do while I was gone? Anything exciting?'

'No.' My voice comes out harsh. I feel bad that I haven't made the time to show her around LA. I know she'd love the farmer's market, or a visit to the beach.

Tatianna and I sit down side by side at the breakfast table—me immersed in an earnings report on my tablet and her filing her nails into little ovals.

I check my calendar for the week ahead and remind Tatianna about our upcoming trip. 'We leave for Paris on Monday.'

She turns to me suddenly. 'I can't go. I have a shoot in New York on Monday and Tuesday.'

'What are you talking about? We've had this trip planned for three months.' I've been courting an international investor and would be meeting him face to face in Paris where Tatianna and I were supposed to be entertaining him and his wife all week.

'Sorry, but there's no way I'm canceling,' she says. 'I've wanted to work with this designer ever since I saw his adorable line of fuzzy boots last fall.'

'You wouldn't have to cancel it if you hadn't booked over our trip in the first place.'

She huffs in frustration.

'I need to be able to count on you,' I say.

'And I need you to support my modeling career,' she bites back.

'When have I not supported you?'

She glares at me, her eyes searching mine, but doesn't respond.

Our conversation is far from over, but I need to get my emotions under control before I do something hasty.

Chapter Ten

Mia

Yesterday's drinking combined with my inability to sleep last night makes sleeping in all morning sound like a great option. I lie with my eyes closed in the overstuffed bed. It's like lying in a cloud. I stretch my arms and legs, letting the smooth sheets caress my skin. No matter how far I stretch in any direction, I can't reach the edge of the bed. Such an expanse of luxury shouldn't make for a rough night's sleep.

The words 'rough night' doesn't even begin to cover the roller-coaster of emotions I experienced last night. My eyes blink open as I remember the cause of the unrest. This morning Collins said we would talk. I can only assume we're finally going to have a conversation about our twenty-year marriage proposal.

Part of me wants to think positive. Maybe the reason he wants to talk is because he's decided he wants me in his life. My pulse races with excitement at the idea, and I pull off the sheets, and I head for the shower.

The water is nice and hot, and I take my time, scrubbing myself from head to toe. If he does want to be with me, will he kiss me again? Will it have all the heat and passion of our stolen kiss in the ocean? I shave my underarms, my legs, and my bikini area. If we shared such a kiss, would it lead to more? Another night alone with him on a boat. Being alone with him—anywhere. My pulse races.

Of course, it will never be as easy as that. He will have to settle things with Tatianna first. So maybe we won't be able to be together right away, maybe he'll ask me to give him time to break things off with Tatianna. They've been together long enough, and she deserves to be let down first. And it's the right thing to do.

I step out of the shower and dry myself off with an overly fluffy towel.

As I finish running my flat iron through my hair, putting the finishing touches on my carefully crafted, *ready to have a serious talk with the man of my dreams* look, the other possibility rears its evil head, filling my stomach with a cold and twisty dread. It's the more realistic option.

Damn reality. I hate it.

But I know it's the more likely outcome of our talk. He's said it already: his life is complicated now. 'We can't just pinky swear and then live happily ever after.' I feel my shoulders slump, and I stare at my sad reflection in the bathroom mirror.

He'll tell me he's sorry, but that it can't work between us. Collins will be nice about it, because he has always been good to me. But he'll ask that—because it's awkward and all—I find a job and move out as soon as I can.

He'll ask me if I'm okay.

Somehow, I'll force a nod. I'll manage to get away from him before I curl up in a ball and cry. Collins will come and find me, and I'll convince him that everything is fine. Just like all of our little fights and misunderstandings over the years.

I take a deep breath and check myself one last time in the mirror and fix a stray hair—not exactly sure why I bother—before heading out to find Collins. As I take the stairs, I wonder if it really has to be that way. Because after all this time—after the insanity of me flying across the country to make good on this silly promise—he could have laughed it off. He could have just pretended the whole thing was some stupid joke. And frankly, I'm so embarrassed by it that I would probably have gone along with it.

But he didn't laugh it off. He asked to talk about it. So now, here I am, half trembling, half giddy, and all messed up. I head down the hall to the kitchen, where I know he takes his breakfast. Either he's about to crush me, or give me hope this isn't over yet.

Option C. None of the above.

I enter the kitchen to find Tatianna home early from her shoot. She sits next to Collins at the breakfast table filing her nails while he works at his computer. I struggle to hide my disappointment. *Crap.*

She sits so straight in her chair, it's as if she's got an iron rod shoved up her hooha. When did she get back? My jaw tenses, but when my eyes move from her to Collins my anger fades, and is replaced with concern. Collins looks exhausted. His eyes narrow and his shoulders hunch up as if the very act of being awake is painful. He also looks angry, but about what, I have no idea. Neither of them hear me enter, and are both still lost in their tasks.

'Collins,' I say.

He looks up and tries to smile, but his brow wrinkles. His gaze roams over my body, and he freezes. I wonder if he's angry about something, or maybe appreciating the extra time and care I took getting ready. I help myself to a cup of coffee and take a seat across from them.

'Are you okay?' I ask.

He leans his chin heavily on his hand and says, 'I had one, maybe two, too many scotches last night.'

My face heats as I remember our texts last night. Had he been so drunk he didn't know what he was saying? My heart sinks. He probably doesn't even remember. It's all there in your text history, I want to say. We're supposed to have our talk today.

Tatianna looks up. 'Morning, Mia. Did you sleep well?'

'Yeah,' I lie and force a smile. 'You're back.'

She pokes at an empty bowl in front of her. 'We got everything done early. For once.' She looks around. 'Is there anymore cut fruit?' She must be asking one of the staff, but figures out there isn't anyone here to serve her, and gets up, heading to the fridge.

'I didn't forget,' Collins whispers once she's out of earshot.

His words fill me with hope, and I search for any clue on his face of what he's thinking. But I can't read him.

'Meet me out back by the row of palm trees in one hour,' he adds, looking into my eyes with such intensity I feel it deep in my gut. The tension is so thick between us, I think it would be so obvious, but Tatianna is oblivious.

He takes a sip of his coffee, then in a relaxed voice says. 'Any big plans for today?'

'More job hunting.' I shrug.

Tatianna comes back to the table with a peeled banana. 'Maybe Collins will have something for you.'

Collins looks at me and some of his tense mood falls away. 'Sure. I'll check with Suzanna in HR and see what we have open for someone as talented as you.' He's looking at my lips in a way that makes me feel dirty as he says this.

I take a deep breath and it shudders out. 'That would be great, but I don't expect a job just handed to me.' I bite my lip.

Tatianna turns to Collins. 'You know, babe, I have some pretty great talents too.' She opens her mouth and shoves the entire banana in. It's meant to be sexy, but it's too big for her mouth and she struggles to chew it down without choking on it.

I take a sip of my coffee in an effort to hide my smile. But Collins watches her thoughtfully, then looks at me and smiles, planting both his hands on the table as if he's about to stand. 'Well, sorry to leave you to eat alone, but Tatianna and I have some things to take care of before I head out.'

'Oh. Sure,' I say. *Things? What things? And what about our talk?*

But Collins' expression is blank and tells me nothing. Damn his poker face.

Tatianna's face is talking enough for both of them, though. Her screw-me eyes are drilling a hole all the way through Collins' head and into the wall behind him. She slips her arm up his chest, hooking her hand around his neck. I try to turn away, but find my eyes glued to them in some sort of sick envious gape.

He stands up. 'Good luck with the job hunt. I'll see you later.' Tatianna gets up and follows him out of the room leaving me alone in the kitchen. I glance around the large room blankly and realize I'm no longer hungry.

My face is getting hot. I'm angry.

He said we were going to talk this morning. 'Meet me in an hour,' he said. Well if he thinks I'm going to wait around while he screws his girlfriend, he must be confusing me with some push over. I scoot out of my chair, get up, and find myself storming back up the steps to my room.

By the time I reach my room, my vision is all blurry. I wipe away tears as I close the door and drop down on the bed. How had I allowed myself to get so worked up? I think back to how Sophie said Colton thought Collins loved me. I hadn't meant to, but I must have grabbed on to that. It had snuck its way into my subconscious, and made me think I had a shot, that happily-ever-afters do exist.

Hell, it isn't just that. He led me to think I have a shot. What other reason do we have to talk? If he isn't interested, then there isn't anything to talk about, so why does he want to talk?

But this question no longer matters. I have all the answers I need in the form of him currently screwing his girlfriend.

Why else did they need to suddenly retreat to the bedroom alone together?

I stand up and find my suitcase, and open it on the bed. The answer is finally forcing its way through my thick skull.

It's time to go home.

Chapter Eleven

Collins

I follow Tatianna upstairs, intent on finishing our conversation. Her little stunt with the banana tells me she thinks we're coming up here to sweep everything under the rug.

When we enter our bedroom, I close and lock the door. She turns to me, smiling, not at all in tune with how frustrated I am. As if to avoid any further discussion, Tatianna pulls her tank top over her head and shimmies out of her shorts.

'What the hell are you doing?' I ask.

'I've been away for two days, and now we're about to be separated again. I thought that's why you wanted to come upstairs.'

Before she can unclasp her bra, I stop her. 'No. I want to talk. Sit down.' I gesture to the bed, and Tatianna reluctantly sits on the edge of it. I hand her the shirt she just took off and watch as she puts it back on. Her eyes latch onto mine, and her smile fades. I don't have time for her games right now. She's used to pouting her lip and getting whatever she wants.

'Where is this going, Tatianna? You and me?'

'What…what do you mean?' she asks, looking confused.

I've never posed a question like this before, never talked of our future, but I think maybe it's time. 'I think we need to discuss this relationship. What do you want out of this? What are your goals?' I ask.

'My goals?' She chews on her lip. 'I don't know, to be on the cover of *InStyle* magazine, to walk all the biggest shows in New York and Milan fashion week next year.'

For the first time in my life, I feel a hole inside of me. A hole that deepens and grows larger with each passing heartbeat. Booking over our trip to Paris only reinforces the fact that I don't rank on her list of priorities. Her future goals mentioned nothing about me, about us, and only included herself. It's typical Tatianna, but it's starting to really fucking bother me. She has no expectations for the future, and while most bachelors in my position might like the no promises, no attachments arrangement we have, I find that I don't anymore. I want to hear her say she can't live without me and that she needs me. We've been together for several years now, and things shouldn't be quite so casual between us. We've never even said I love you. I look her over, taking in the way her long blonde hair falls nearly to her waist, her almond shaped blue eyes, and painted red lips. I care about her—I would hate to see any harm come to her. However, I worry that I don't feel as strongly as I should. We've been dating long enough that I should know by now if I love her.

When Mia looks at me, I feel more heat and emotion between us than I do between me and my girlfriend of three years. And Mia's only been back in my life a handful of days. That realization causes something within me to stir. This disconnect that's been building between Tatianna and me rises to the surfaces and demands attention. I want more. A lot fucking more. I mean, there has to be more than this, right? Mia's hope-filled eyes told me there was—if I'm man enough to embrace it. My life has been devoid of emotion for the last several years as my attention has been focused on growing my business, and yes, I've had my needs met with a warm, willing female to share my bed, but it's lacked any real intimacy.

Tatianna is watching me with a pouted lip, obviously wondering if I've lost my mind. She doesn't get it. She doesn't get me either. That would involve looking outside herself, which she never does.

Mia picked right up on my tense mood this morning in the kitchen, asking me if I was okay. I blamed it on last night's scotch, but the truth was ever since she walked back into my life, looking downright sinful, my head has been spinning.

I sit down on the bed a few feet from Tatianna and consider taking her hand, but we aren't really the hand holding type, so instead I run my palm across the back of my neck.

'Look, Tatianna...' I start, but am at a loss for words. For the first time in my life. I need to tell her what I want. The problem is, I'm not sure I fucking know what that is.

In the week ahead, we'll be on different continents, perhaps now is the time to take a break and consider the future of this relationship. I have no idea how she's going to take this, but it has to be done.

'I want us to both take this week to think about our relationship and what we each want. When I get back from Paris, we'll make a decision about our future.'

'Why does that sound so depressing?' she asks.

'Don't you think it's strange that after three years of dating, we've never examined where this was going?'

'I like being with you,' she says, trying to smooth things over. 'Why mess with a good thing?'

Except this wasn't a good thing anymore, at least not for me. But dealing with my relationship status means I'll have to face my future with Mia. Am I ready for that? Fuck, she's a friend and I wouldn't want to wreck that. I'd definitely need this week to consider where I was headed and with whom. I've never even considered marriage with my girlfriend of three years, and Mia's back in my life for a week and I'm rearranging everything just to keep her here. That speaks volumes. 'I'm going to ask Mia to join me in Paris,' I say.

'I don't have anything to worry about with her, do I?' Tatianna asks, her eyes narrowing on mine.

I shake my head, unable to put into words all that's running through my brain.

Tatianna rises from the bed and steps closer. 'We're good together, Collins. You know we are.' She reaches down and grabs onto my crotch, rubbing lightly. My dick doesn't respond.

'Don't,' I warn.

She shakes her head. 'Take this week, and think things over if you want. But I will be here when you get back.' Her hand curls around my cock, squeezing lightly. 'And don't let her lay a finger on this.'

I rise from the bed and stand there, unsure if there's anything more to say.

Tatianna plays with the long tresses of her hair, and the stack of diamond bangles I bought her clink together on her forearm. She doesn't seem the least bit upset.

'I need to go talk to Mia,' I say and head for the door.

Chapter Twelve

Mia

Other than the airfare and the cab ride to Collins' house, I haven't purchased a thing since I got here. So why won't my goddamn bag close? I put both my forearms on the top of my suitcase and lean all my weight on it, but there are still several inches between the zipper's teeth. I'll never get this thing closed.

'Shoot,' I say aloud and lean back to flip the case open again.

Right on top is my old scrapbook. It's thick, bursting with photos, clippings and other keepsakes. I plop down next to my bag on the bed and leaf through it. It's filled with mementos from my childhood. I'd never meant for it to be a history of my friendship with Collins, but now I see that it is. We were best friends for so long that I guess it makes sense.

Photos of Collins and me goofing off at the county fair, age six.

Collins and me laughing our butts off in his parents' pool, age eight.

Ticket stubs from our first live concert, which he purchased for my thirteenth birthday.

The picture of the lavender wedding dress. I pause at the photo. Such an elegant dress, silk with just a hint of lace.

Now, none of this matters. An entire history wiped away because Collins doesn't have the time to talk to me. He can't even get through breakfast without running off to screw his supermodel girlfriend. He obviously doesn't care, so why should I?

I slam the book closed and hurl the stupid thing at the door, but miss. It strikes the wall with a *whap*, then falls to the floor. The bedroom door bursts open, and Collins pokes his head in, looking worried. 'Mia?' he says. 'Sorry, I was just outside and I heard a loud noise.' He opens the door all the way and looks at me.

My arms are folded as I sit on the bed and glare at the scrapbook lying on the floor. He follows my gaze down, then looks back at me and takes a step inside the room.

'What's wrong?' He looks past me at my suitcase. 'Are you leaving?'

I bite my lip, knowing that I don't have any right to be mad at him. Yet I am. 'Did you have fun with Tatianna?' I ask, realizing I sound like a crazy chick, but not caring. Because he's the one who said we should talk. So now I'm ready. Let's put it all out there. Let's *talk*.

He looks thoughtful for a moment. 'What are you...? Mia, do you think I just ... with Tatianna?' He can't bring himself to say it, but he doesn't have to.

I see in his eyes that he knows what I was thinking. I can also tell from the look on his face that he did *not* just have sex with Tatianna. I go from feeling angry to feeling like an idiot and a jerk.

I cover my face with my hands. 'Collins, I'm sorry. I'm a freaking mess.'

He picks up my discarded scrapbook and carries it over, sitting next to me on the bed. 'Silly Gremlin.' He nudges me with his shoulder. 'Always letting your imagination run wild.'

I cross my legs and turn to face him on the bed. 'I can't help it. Whenever we're together, I guess I get a little carried away.'

He chuckles and takes my hand. The touch sends warmth all the way up my arm. 'You aren't the only one affected when we're together.' He glances at my mouth, then meets my gaze. I lick my lips. He's just inches away, and I think he's about to kiss me. I want him to lean down and close the distance, but he forces his eyes closed and takes a deep breath. When he opens them, he moves a bit away from me, but doesn't let go of my hand, squeezing it instead.

He waits a beat before he continues. 'I'm sorry I kissed you in the water that day.'

'Why?' I ask, even though I know.

'It's not that I didn't enjoy the kiss.' His voice goes low, and I wonder if he's reliving the moment. 'I just don't think it was fair to you. I'm with Tatianna.'

I feel a stab of pain as his words hit me. 'I see.' I nod and let go of his hand. 'You've got Tatianna now. I'm no supermodel, and if you want that, I can't compete with her.' I stand up and begin to refold my clothes. It's definitely time to go.

'Hey, stop packing.' He puts his hands over mine to stop me. 'Where are you going?'

'I don't know,' I say. But I stop packing.

'As for my relationship with Tatianna, I'm not sure if she and I still want the same things. We just had a talk about where things were heading with us.' He runs his hand along the back of his neck. 'I need to take some time and think things through.'

I feel a glimmer of hope at his words. The idea of Collins breaking it off with Tatianna, of him being single, should be exciting. But as I search his eyes I see that this is hard for him. It could be that he's not ready to leave her, or that he's just frustrated because he's not sure what he wants. Either way, his unhappy state doesn't allow me to take pleasure in this news. At least not a lot.

'But about our promise.' His brow furrows and I hold my breath wanting to know, but also terrified. 'I'm just not sure...' He trails off. But I don't need him to finish the sentence. I know what he's saying.

'Then why even bring it up again?' I ask. 'What is there to talk about?'

He scoots closer and reaches for my hand, but thinks better of it. 'You being here, Mia, suddenly back in my life. It's a lot to process. And marriage…' He makes a cursing sound under his breath.

'It's fine,' I interrupt. 'It was a stupid childhood promise. It doesn't mean anything.' My voice shakes over the last words and I suck in a quick inhale. I won't let myself cry in front of him.

This time he does take my hand, pressing his palm against mine. 'Gremlin?'

My eyes lift to his.

'I don't want you to go anywhere. I lost you once when I was fifteen, and I'm not ready to let you go again. Stay. Please. As long as you want. As long as you need to.'

'But won't it be weird with Tatianna? Doesn't she think it's weird?'

'You're my best friend, Mia. There's nothing weird about you being here. Besides, this is my house. I decide who stays and how long.' He narrows his eyes as he looks at me, and pokes me in the arm. 'You stay as long as you want.'

'Fine,' I say. A smile finds its way to my lips. He can't poke me like that, the way he did when he…

I'm not happy with the way our talk has gone, but the fact that he doesn't want me gone is something. And honestly, I still don't have anywhere else to go, so it's also a relief.

'Good,' he says. 'Don't unpack. I want you to come to Paris with me Monday. Tatianna backed out, and I already made travel plans for two.' He explains that it's a business trip he's been planning and that she has a shoot. His eyes fill with irritation as he talks about her last minute cancelation. It's frustrating to watch how little regard she has for him.

It only takes me a second to nod my assent. 'Paris? Of course.' I'd do anything for him, and convincing me to go to Europe on a free trip wasn't exactly a hardship.

'What's this?' He pulls my scrapbook onto his lap and opens it. He chuckles into his fist, his eyes growing warm. 'I can't believe you still have *The Gremlin Files*. I'm so glad you brought this.' I blush at the silly name he has for my scrapbook. I sit down next to him and he leans in so that I can see as he leafs through the pages. His arm brushes against mine and I revel in the heat coming from his touch. I try to tell myself this touch is innocent. We were best friends as children, we could be just friends again. But as my body leans in next to his, I know there's nothing just friends about the way I want to nuzzle my nose along his jaw line and inhale his scent.

At each new page, we gasp and laugh, remembering the past and all the wonderful memories.

He pauses on the page with the ticket stubs to our first concert. 'This was the best show. This book is great. Can I borrow it?'

'Sure.' I shrug.

'Look, I have to go take care of a few things for work, but I'm so glad you're coming to Paris.' He steps out, and closes the door behind him.

I'm glad I'm going too.

I know the right thing to do is give him the space he needs to think about his relationship with Tatianna. But spending a whole week alone with him in a romantic city like Paris? The temptation will be nearly overwhelming.

Chapter Thirteen

Collins

When we arrive in Paris, the joy on Mia's face is incredible. She's like a little kid in a candy shop, her eyes wide and her mouth curled into a silly grin. I can't help getting swept up in her excitement, my own mood lightening despite having been here many times. Even after a twelve-hour flight, she's full of energy and ready to explore.

'Where are we going first?' she asks, as the driver cruises down the highway that leads from the airport to the city.

'The hotel.' I chuckle at her. 'I thought we could drop our luggage, and then I'll show you around a little, but we have a business dinner in a couple of hours.'

'Okay.'

On the plane ride here, I told her all about Pierre and the successful European firm he runs. I would like to take over managing his company's investments stateside and need to show him why that would benefit him. But first I need to win him over. The French are much more relational when it comes to business. They don't get in bed with just anyone. His wife's name is Adele, and I explained that I needed Mia to keep her happy and occupied. Happy wife, happy life, and all that. I know by tonight we will both have our game faces on, but for now, I'm happy to indulge her in the role of tour guide.

When we reach the hotel and step into the opulent marble lobby, Mia's eyes dart over the elegant paintings and the finely upholstered furniture. I stand at the check-in counter, waiting, as the clerk types something on the keyboard.

'Monsieur, the luxury king suite you've requested has been prepared. The bellhop will bring your luggage up.'

Shit. My assistant booked the room for me and Tatianna months ago, of course it's just one room—with one bed. 'Actually, I need a bigger suite—something with two bedrooms.'

She looks down at the monitor and begins typing again. 'I'm sorry, but we're completely full at the moment.' She frowns.

'Okay, then just a regular room with two beds?'

She shakes her head. 'We have no occupancy other than the suite you reserved.' She explains that there's some big fashion convention happening this week and many of the hotels are full.

I consider searching for another hotel, one outside the city, but with my meetings all being in the business district, I realize that's silly. Mia and I are adults. We will be fine sharing a room. Shit, we used to have sleepovers all the time when we were little.

'Fine,' I say to the clerk. 'Please send up our bags.'

I find Mia admiring an oil painting at the far end of the lobby.

'The colors are amazing,' she says when I get close.

I love how she can find such simple joy in things. I realize if I was here with Tatianna, she'd probably be complaining that our room wasn't quite ready and her nose would be stuck in her phone.

'I have some news,' I say, guiding her toward the elevator with my hand at the small of her back.

'What's that?'

'The reservation was made months ago by my assistant, and now the hotel is completely full.'

Her eyebrows draw up. 'So? Spit it out, Collins.'

'How do you feel about sharing a bed?'

'Oh.' She lets out a nervous laugh and staggers back a step, her hand curling around the railing inside the elevator, like she needs the support to remain upright.

Before she has time to respond, the doors open to our floor. We walk in silence to the room, and I slide the key card into the slot beside the door.

'It'll be fine,' I assure her, motioning her to enter ahead of me.

'Of course,' she says.

My stomach tightens into a knot, because the moment the door closes, and I'm alone with Mia, all I want to do is throw her down on the bed and kiss the living daylights out of her. Perhaps it was our close proximity on the plane, the way she rested her head on my shoulder while she slept, or that I feel closer and more connected to her than I have any right to. She's not mine. But shit, I want to feel her hot mouth on mine and soft body in my hands.

Shit.

Memories float into my brain, how her body felt under mine the first time we had sex, how her tight pussy fit me like a hot glove… No one has ever felt as good. Even though it was our first time, and it was little awkward, it was still the best, because it was not just physical, it was life changing, it was with the one person who had no hidden agendas, it was just two people with real feelings, exploring each other. I would kill for another chance like that.

A knock at the door interrupts my wicked thoughts, and I tip the bellhop after he delivers our suitcases.

Clearing my throat, I mumble something about cleaning up and head to the bathroom.

Christ, how am I supposed to survive an entire week sleeping beside Mia, watching her emerge pink and damp from the shower, listening to her sleepy sounds as she drifts off, being surrounded by her scent…

I scrub my hands over my face. I feel like an awkward teenager. So I do the only thing I can think to do. I grab a squirt of body wash and begin jacking myself off.

My hand slides up and down and as hot water pelts against my back. I close my eyes and lose myself in the moment, pumping my fist over my cock in eager strokes. When I picture Mia's round ass and lush tits I come so hard I have to fight to suppress the groan crawling up my throat.

When I emerge from the bathroom with a white towel secured around my hips, Mia is sitting in the center of the bed with a map of Paris unfolded in front of her.

'Plotting out your route?' I ask, grabbing my suitcase.

She looks up, sees my undressed state, and her eyes widen in surprise. 'Uh-huh,' she mumbles.

'Sorry, I'll get dressed in the bathroom, I just need to grab my clothes.'

After I'm changed, we head out into the sunlight, Mia snapping photos of every cathedral and fountain with her camera phone, and talking excitedly about how cute the quaint cobblestone streets and cafes are. I'm at ease in her presence, and I'm able to just relax before the big meeting tonight.

We stop at a patisserie, and I buy her a coffee and a chocolate croissant, ordering in French, something I've done a million times before, but the way Mia's raises both eyebrows, you'd think I'd just flown to the moon.

'Why didn't I take French in school?' she says. 'It sounds so elegant.'

Then she sinks her teeth into the flaky pastry crust and moans as she chews. There's something Tatianna would never do.

'Dear God, taste this!' she says shoving the pastry toward me.

I chuckle, but decide to humor her, biting into the other side of the treat. 'Damn, that is good.'

After our little outing, we don't have much time before dinner, so we head back to the hotel. We change into our eveningwear, and when Mia emerges from the bathroom, I almost swallow my damn tongue.

'Is this okay?' she asks.

She's in a strapless black gown that falls all the way to the floor. The bottom half is loose and swishy, but the top is form fitting and the modest peek of cleavage makes me want to see more.

'That's fine,' I bark out. I clench my jaw and fight the urge to adjust myself.

She frowns and runs her hand over the fabric. 'I could change…'

I stand in front of her and place my hands on her bare shoulders. 'You look beautiful,' I say, my tone softening. 'Don't change. You're perfect.'

'Thank you,' she whispers, her eyes latched onto mine. 'You look amazing too.'

Without my consent, my thumb begins skittering back and forth along her skin, rubbing little circles along her collarbone. 'You're so soft.'

She offers me a small smile. 'I'm kind of obsessed with body lotion.'

I smile down at her. 'Are you ready for tonight? You remember everything I told you about Pierre and his wife?'

She nods. 'Of course. It's going to go great, don't worry, Coll.'

She grabs her handbag and we head toward the elevator. All I want to do is cop a feel and attack her in the hotel suite, but I'm trying to be on my best behavior. I'm technically still with Tatianna and I won't betray that. I'm not a cheater, and I wouldn't want to start a relationship with Mia that way anyway. The look in her eyes tells me that if I did make a move, she wouldn't stop me. That information is dangerous.

We arrive at the restaurant early, so I guide Mia toward the bar. 'Would you like to grab a drink first?'

'Sure,' she says, lifting up on her toes to slide onto the bar stool gracefully.

She's so easy going and up for anything, it calms me, even though I'm about to negotiate a thirty million dollar deal with a man whose first language isn't English.

When I'd discovered her packing up her suitcase two days ago, ready to flee for home, something inside me snapped. I knew I couldn't let her go. I realized in that moment that if I lost Mia again, I lost my connection to the past. And I don't want that. I've barely been living these past few years. Sure, I've been going through the motions, but there's been no real joy in it. Sitting here with her, watching her swirl the ruby-colored wine in her glass, I know I've made the right call bringing her with me.

We enjoy a glass of wine together, Mia's eyes floating over the bar and restaurant.

'Collins?' she asks.

'Hmm?'

'Will you help me order if the menu is in French?'

'Of course,' I say, taking her hand.

She smiles up at me. 'Don't worry. You've got this.'

I smile, despite my nerves. On the outside no one would know I'm tense and anxious. I always get this way before a big deal, but my colleagues have always applauded my ability to remain calm and collected. Only Mia knows me too well. She sees straight through me, to the man inside and somehow she knows tonight is important to me.

We finish our wine and head back to the hostess stand. Pierre has just arrived. I recognize him from the headshot on his company's website.

'It's show time, baby,' I say to Mia, taking her hand and guiding her to the front of the restaurant.

'Monsieur Ducharme,' I say, stopping directly in front of him.

'Ah, Collins Drake,' he says, his voice deep and heavily accented. 'Please call me Pierre.'

We shake hands, our grips firm and our eyes centered on each other's. There are a million nuisances that pass between us at the seemingly innocuous handshake. His eyes implore mine, as if to inquire if I'm as good as he's heard. And I give an imperceptible nod, as if to say fuck yeah I am.

We release hands, and Mia surprises me by lifting up on her toes and air kissing each of Pierre's cheeks, as is the French custom.

'Pierre, I'm Mia. Collins has told me many wonderful things about the success of your company. It's my pleasure to meet you.'

He looks down at Mia, and his mouth curls into a grin. 'Mia, *c'est tres jolie*. Beautiful name,' he says. He introduces us to Adele and Mia treats her to the same greeting and compliments her dress. They are soon chatting happily as the hostess leads us further into the restaurant and seats us at a table in the back.

There's a moment of stillness, as a quiet hesitation falls over our group. The four of us are relative strangers. As I regroup and gather my thoughts, Mia, the sweet and thoughtful girl that she is, pays a compliment to their beautiful home country. This seems to break the ice. I listen as Mia asks thoughtful questions about art, history, local customs and the French parliament. She is hungry for knowledge and a great conversationalist. Pierre leans forward on his elbows, immediately riveted with this beautiful, intelligent woman. Adele and I exchange polite smiles, and I ask about her work. She teaches at the university—finance. I smile, knowing her and Mia will also have much to discuss when Pierre and I retreat to the lounge with a cigar later to talk business.

Throughout dinner Mia continues to impress me. Not only is she stunning in that floor-length dress, but she's professional, polished, excellent at making small talk, and sets everyone at ease. It's very unlike taking Tatianna to events like this. Being in the presence of a supermodel makes everyone uncomfortable—from the women wanting to drive a pitchfork through her skinny body to the men eye-fucking her all night. It was always a headache. This is refreshing and nice.

Polishing off the last bite of my meal, I realize this has been *fun*. In a way that most business dinners are not. We argued over the absurd trends in American music and laughed at the silly childhood stories Mia told. The wine flowed easily throughout dinner, though I limited myself to two glasses so I'm clear-headed, and I noticed Mia doing the same. Politely accepting each glass Pierre offered her, but taking small sips of water in between.

I don't know what will happen tonight when we're alone and slightly tipsy from the wine. All I know is that I want to be alone with her. I can't help my eyes watching her mouth when she speaks, or from falling down to the front of her dress where her breasts are nestled so enticingly. There is only one thing standing in the way of me and Mia heading back to our hotel—the business I need to settle with Pierre.

'Shall we.' I meet his eyes and gesture toward the back rooms.

He nods. 'Yes, let's.'

I lean down and my lips brush past Mia's cheek. 'You are amazing,' I whisper. 'Will you be okay?'

She glances up at me, playfully. 'Go get 'em, tiger.'

I laugh, despite myself. Confidence surges through me and I give a tight nod.

As I lead Pierre away to the lounge, I can feel Mia's eyes on me the entire time, sending warm darts of pleasure zipping through me.

Chapter Fourteen

Mia

This evening is important to Collins. It's not that he needs this deal, obviously, for Collins it's more about the challenge. I can see it in his eyes; this is a big one. He wants this deal. And what Collins wants, he gets. Going out to dinner with him and his prospect made me nervous as hell, but I refused to be the reason for failure, so I swallowed my fear, and dove into the challenge with him. Dinner was amazing. I was worried Pierre and Adele would spend the evening looking down their noses at me, but they proved that although they are billionaires, they're still human. They humored me, and all my prying questions, and even let me go on telling silly stories about Collins as a kid.

By the time Collins and Pierre excuse themselves to talk business, I've begun to really like the French couple. My eyes follow Collins as the men head back to the lounge. I can't help but wonder, as I watch his confident yet relaxed stride, if in another life--one where my parent's hadn't had to move us when I was a teenager--I would be here as Collins' wife. Pierre and Adele would make great couple-friends with us in that alternate reality.

'You are an accountant, no?' Adele asks, pulling my attention back to the present, true reality.

'No,' I say. 'Yes,' I add. I laugh, unable to believe I've held it together the whole evening, only to be tripped up with a yes or no question. 'I have been. I'm between jobs. You are an economics professor, right?' My question smoothly directs her attention away from my complex and undesirable situation, and guides her into discussing the differences in European economic structures.

She manages to talk for over an hour on the topic. We order another bottle of wine and, as a money geek, I am fascinated to hear how the cultural differences have woven their way into her theoretical framework.

'I'm sorry,' she stops herself. 'I didn't mean to go on about this for so long. It's just such a nice surprise that you have a finance background.' She takes a sip of her wine. 'Pierre had the impression you were a model or something like that. I admit, I was a bit worried we wouldn't have anything to talk about. I'm so glad I was wrong.'

'Are you kidding? I could talk about this stuff all night,' I say genuinely. It feels great knowing that I'm doing my part, or at least I'm not messing it up too miserably. I also can't help but mark down a score for Team Mia that Tatianna wouldn't have fared as well if she'd come.

Adele takes a sip of her wine, then looks over at the door leading to the private lounges. The door the men went through to talk about their business deal. She smiles warmly at me and says, 'Your husband, Collins, is a very nice man. You are a lucky woman.'

'Oh, no,' I say. 'We aren't married.' God, if only.

'But you've been together a long time, no?'

I shake my head. 'No. We're just friends.' The words sting my eyes a little. The truth sucks. I take a sip of my wine and tell myself to hold it together. I don't want to make this night about me, I'm supposed to be entertaining Adele. Keeping her happy.

Adele leans forward and puts her hand on my arm, narrowing her eyes. '*Non,*' she insists. 'Surely you are together. I see the way you are. Your bodies know each other. And the way he looks at you...' She flicks her wrist as if it's a done deal and she has just, in fact, married us. Then she holds up her glass to me--a wordless toast.

Her over-dramatic zeal makes me laugh. I can't help it. I clink glasses with her and take a sip. Still, maybe there is something to what she says. If someone who's just met us thinks we've been together for years... I recall Sophie telling me that Collins is in love with me, and now this comment from a practical stranger.

The way he's been looking at me all night, though. It's hard to catch it because he's very skilled at guarding his emotions, but I'd seen it. Maybe she'd picked up on it too. Several times I caught him staring at me, his eyes filled with encouragement and interest. But his look also drifted down my neck on occasion. A look that sent tingles through my body. A look that made me cross my legs and savor that delicious throbbing. The looks got more intense as the night went on, and the last look he'd given me before he went to talk business with Pierre. That parting look said so much. Don't move. I'll deal with you later.

I swirl the last of my wine in my glass and wonder if it isn't obvious to everyone. Am I looking at him with the same hunger? I don't know how I can hide it.

Collins and Pierre burst out of the back rooms with their arms slung around each other's shoulders like they've been drinking buddies forever, and singing some French song. Well, shouting the words to the song, anyway.

The expression on Collins' face is slightly guarded, which is the only way I can tell he isn't fully inebriated, but there's a sparkle in his eye, and he's smiling.

It doesn't take a Ph.D. to know they've decided to work together.

When Collins' eyes meet mine, he continues singing, but swoops towards me and slides his arm around my waist, pulling me to my feet. He leans toward my ear, whispering, '*Je t'aime, mon ange*.' His breath on my neck sends heat through me. I have no clue what the words mean, but it doesn't matter. If we were alone my dress would be in a pile on the floor right now. I take a deep shaky breath in effort to maintain control, but it's no use. With him so close, I can smell the sweet cigar smoke and bourbon on his breath. A combination so masculine. My body leans into his without my permission. My arms circle his neck. Our eyes lock. My heart is beating faster than humanly possible. His jaw tightens as if he's fighting the urge to pounce.

'*Follement amoureux*,' Adele says under her breath.

I don't know what it means, but Collins seems to. He looks over to Adele and Pierre who are on their feet as well. Collins loosens his grip around my waist, standing up a bit straighter. As if he's just remembered that we aren't alone. God, I long for the moment when we will be alone together.

I bite my lip and force myself to look away from Collins, smiling once more at our dinner companions. Adele pulls on her shawl, Collins takes care of the tab, and we say our goodbyes. Then we are alone. Collins' arm on the small of my back guides me out of the restaurant onto the dimly lit Paris streets.

'There's a taxi stand.' Collins' voice is low and he speaks in my ear. The taxi stand is several blocks down, and he puts a protective arm around me as we walk. For the first time in my life, I find myself tongue-tied. The only thing I can think about is Collins. It's like a highlight reel. Collins' wet body pressed against my bare chest in the ocean. His hot kisses. The image of him today exiting the hotel shower this afternoon with only a towel wrapped around his waist. His tan sculpted chest still had a few droplets of water clinging to it. I wanted to help dry him off. Hell, I want to shower with him.

Again I find myself leaning into him, pressing the side of my body to his as we walk.

The streetlights give the city a rose hue. Collins looks so good with his tailored suit and tie. It's like a dream. I keep on expecting to wake up in my old apartment back in Connecticut.

'Did you and Pierre make a deal?' I ask.

'We did.' His face is relaxed and happy, like I haven't seen him in a while. 'Thank you, you were perfect,' he says, pressing a quick kiss to my temple as we walk.

At the taxi stand, Collins helps me into the car, following close behind me. The small dome light of the cab shows me the look on his face. There is so much hunger in his eyes.

'What did you say to me back at the restaurant?' I ask, my head feeling like I'm in a fog.

He takes a moment to consider my question. 'My angel,' he says softly and I wonder if I'm getting the whole truth.

'And what did Adele say to us before we left?'

'Crazy in love,' he says, looking directly into my eyes.

My stomach does a little flip and desire pools at the base of my spine, sending pleasurable tingles into my lower half.

The driver better step on it. And if this really is a dream, just please don't let me wake up yet.

Chapter Fifteen

Collins

On the cab ride back to the hotel, I can't stop my eyes from lingering on Mia's, or my hands from finding hers in the darkened interior. She was amazing tonight. I'm unsure what will happen once we reach the hotel and part of me doesn't want this cab ride to end. Uncertainty swims in my gut, making me question everything. My body knows what it wants to happen, it's my head where the uncertainty lies.

I couldn't believe I'd whispered *I love you, my angel* to her at the restaurant. It was in French, so she didn't know what I said, but the honesty to the words surprised me.

We're almost back to our hotel, so I fish my wallet from my pocket and slide out a few bills for the driver. Digging my cell phone out next, a string of texts light up the screen. They are from Colton—from several hours ago. I read each one in quick succession.

I thought Tatianna was with you in Paris.

What's going on man?

I hadn't thought to tell him that I was taking Mia in place of Tatianna. But I don't see why it matters.

Soph and I are at Platinum nightclub, and Tatianna is here— dancing with another man—some dickhead who thinks he's god's gift to women. WTF.

Tatianna is supposed to be in New York, not dancing with God knows who. Even more troubling than that is Colton bothered to message me in the first place. If she was dancing innocently— something good-natured and fun—he wouldn't be texting me. It means that he's alarmed enough by what he saw tonight to alert me. Unease churns inside me.

I stuff my phone back into my pocket as the driver pulls to a stop beside the curb. I'm frustrated and confused, but Mia and I have just shared a great night. I don't want to take this out on her. I hand the driver a wad of money and help Mia from the car.

'Is everything okay?' she asks, sensing the shift in my mood.

'Everything's fine.' At least I'm trying to pretend it is.

She smiles up at me, trying to get my happy mood to return. 'We should be celebrating your big deal. Are you sure you don't want to go out?' she asks.

'I'd rather just go back to the room.'

She nods. 'Me too.'

God, what I want to do to her when we get back to the room. It's like a sweet-torture imagining what she will feel like. But if I fuck Mia tonight, I will be no better than Tatianna, with her lies about being in New York. I have to remind myself that I need to handle one thing at a time. I have to end things with Tatianna, because if and when I take Mia, it will be with a clear conscience.

When we enter the hotel room, the mood is quiet and subdued.

I turn on a lamp, which casts a dim glow in the room, then loosen my tie. Mia bends down and removes her black high heels one at a time, giving me a glimpse of the cleavage that's taunted me all night. All thoughts of Tatianna and the baggage I need to deal with back in LA are pushed from my mind. It's just me and this stunning woman, with whom I share a deep history, alone in a hotel room halfway across the world.

'I'm going to change,' she says, grabbing her overnight bag and heading into the bathroom.

I don't know if it's intentional, but she leaves the bathroom door open just a crack and I'm treated to an erotic show as her fingers slide the zipper slowly down her back and she steps out of the dress. I walk three steps closer to the bathroom, then force myself stop. I want to go to her, but I know I can't. My line of vision is obstructed, but I can see just enough. The push of her breasts over the cups of a lace bra, the string of black silk between her ass cheeks when she turns around. She undoes the clasp of her bra and lets it fall to the floor, then she steps out of the panties, drawing them down her hips slowly, like she's performing a strip tease just for me. My cock hardens and grows in my dress pants, pushing against my zipper. Mia is so beautiful, and she doesn't even know it. A quality that makes her all the more tempting.

She pulls a T-shirt over her head and rejoins me in the bedroom. My head won't let me forget the fact that she doesn't have anything on under that thin T-shirt. I remove my jacket and cufflinks while Mia sits down on the edge of the bed and watches me. The room is too quiet, too full of desire. When I look at her big green eyes, she takes my breath away. They are full of such honesty, I can read her like a book. She wants more. She wants *me*. I'm taken back to that night fifteen years ago when those same emerald eyes were wide and unblinking when she asked me to be her first. It doesn't matter who she's been with since then. I was the first man to be inside of her, and that thought fills me with a strange sense of pride.

'Are you sure this is okay?' I ask, looking from her, to the bed.

She shrugs and offers me a shy smile. 'We used to have sleepovers all the time, remember?'

'Of course I remember. But your mom stopped letting you sleep over the year we turned twelve.'

She laughs. 'Too bad she didn't know that we'd be playing *I'll show you mine if you show me yours* since we were seven.'

I chuckle. God, the things that come out of her mouth kill me. 'That was only once if I recall.'

'Yes, but I remember you asking several times. I only gave in because I was curious. I didn't have brothers. I didn't know what a boy looked like down there.'

'Did I disappoint?'

She smirks, tugging at something inside me. 'I'm quite certain you've never disappointed a female in your life.'

The room is silent for a moment, and I continue undressing, toeing off my shoes and removing my socks.

'You were my first in so many ways,' she says.

I glance over at her, where she's laying back on the bed. 'And you were mine,' I say.

She sighs, wistfully. 'It was a lifetime time ago.'

It feels like just yesterday. I turn away from her, so she can't see the longing in my eyes. I remove my dress shirt and cotton undershirt, leaving me in my boxer briefs momentarily. I grab a pair of loose athletic shorts from my bag and tug them on, then I join her on the bed.

'Thank you for tonight. I'm glad you came with me.'

'You're welcome,' she says. 'I'm glad I'm here. With you.' She reaches out for my hand, it's an innocent gesture, but given the circumstances—her with her bare pussy under that T-shirt, and me shirtless, it's all the invitation I need. My cock hardens visibly, tenting the thin shorts I have on.

'Mia…' My throat constricts, and I fight off a wave of desire. 'I… fuck.' I squeeze her hand and let it go.

Her eyes widen as her gaze travels down my bare chest to my lap, and she chews on her lower lip. 'Collins…' The emotion and longing in her voice are unmistakable. Why in the fuck I thought

I could share a bed with this woman, I have no idea. It's our first night here, and I want to ravage her—fuck her senseless in a thousand different positions until she can no longer stand.

She places her hand flat against my belly and meets my eyes. 'You're aroused,' she says. Her touch is gentle, but I can still feel the heat of her warm palm against my skin. Her honesty is beautiful. Her words are simple, but she always speaks the truth.

'Yes,' I say, hoarsely. 'I'm in bed with a beautiful woman.'

She blinks and her eyes fall from mine. She's never been great at taking a compliment. Placing two fingers under her chin, I lift her face so she's looking at me again. 'You're incredible. The way you were tonight.' I swallow. I have to take a moment to compose myself, otherwise I'm going to admit things that are better kept quiet. 'You're amazing. And I can't lie, you turn me on so much.'

'I want you to kiss me again,' she says, her tongue dampening her lower lip.

'Trust me, I want to.' I clench my fists at my sides. 'I have to deal with…'

'I know,' she interrupts. 'It wouldn't be right.' Her tone is sad, but filled with understanding.

I smile, appreciating that she isn't going to make this any harder than it already is. Actually, if I got any harder, I might spontaneously combust. My balls feel heavy and achy. I need to come.

Lifting one hand to her face, I run my fingertips along her cheek, tracing her cheekbone, her jaw, touching my thumb to her lower lip. I push my thumb into the warmth of her plush lower lip and she makes a small sound of need. She's so aroused, she's practically trembling. She presses her thighs together and her quick inhale of breath tells me the tiny bit of friction was pleasurable. She's wet. I can smell her faint scent, and I want to bury my face between her legs, and lap up every ounce of moisture from her pussy.

My hand resumes caressing her cheek. 'Collins,' she groans, pressing her thighs together.

I recall Tatianna's words during our last conversation. She lightly gripped my cock and said *don't let her lay a finger on this.* A wicked thought invades my mind. If I use my own hand, I won't be breaking my promise. My lust-filled brain knows the logic is all wrong, but none of me cares.

'Will you do something for me?' I ask, my voice breathless.

She nods.

'I want you to touch your pussy,' I whisper.

She sucks in a breath, and her eyes widen.

I push my thumb into her mouth, her lips parting to accept me. Her mouth is hot and wet and when she swirls her tongue around my thumb, I imagine it's the head of my cock and release a strangled groan.

Removing my thumb, I reach down and palm my cock through my shorts. 'Fuck.' My body aches with the need for a release.

When she opens her mouth to speak, I think she's about to argue, to tell me that this is crazy. 'Will you…' her eyes fall to my lap. 'Stroke yourself too?' she asks.

I nod. 'If you rub that swollen clit of yours.' I glance down at her bare legs, which are still pressed together.

She swallows, and her eyes get this determined look. It's beautiful. She lifts her T-shirt, slowly, carefully, treating me to another erotic show.

My greedy gaze follows the path, eating up each inch of skin she exposes. She's shaved bare, and my mouth waters knowing how smooth she'd be against my face. She continues lifting the shirt until she can pull it off over her head. I appreciate the dip in her soft belly, and the way her full, heavy breasts sway when she drops the shirt over the side of the bed.

Once she's naked, she gets a little shy, and I worry for a second that she's going to back out on me.

'Your breasts are beautiful,' I say. 'Touch them for me,' I whisper.

Tentatively, she brings her hands to her breasts and cups their weight.

'Gorgeous,' I murmur, urging her on.

Still unsure, and chewing on her lower lip, her fingertips graze her nipples and she draws a shuddering breath.

'That's it. It's so fucking hot watching you.'

She circles her nipples and they harden into peaks. Her eyes drift closed and she releases a soft sigh from the pleasurable contact.

'Does that feel good, sweetheart?' I ask.

She blinks her eyes open and finds my eyes. 'Yes,' she breathes.

'Good girl. Trail your right hand down your belly.'

With her eyes still on mine, she lowers her hand.

'Slow,' I tell her.

She swallows and slows her movements, letting her fingers graze her belly, then her hip bone as she moves it lower.

'Put your hand between your legs and tell me how wet you are.'

Her fingers dip lower, and she moans. 'I'm soaked, Collins.'

Fuck.

I need to touch my cock, but I won't do it until she asks again. Right now is about her—her pleasure. And something tells me if I'm not directing her movements, encouraging her, she'll stop. I can't have that.

'Push one finger inside for me,' I growl.

She does, sinking her finger in up to the knuckle, and lets out a moan as her eyes drift closed.

'Tell me how you feel,' I whisper.

She inhales sharply, her finger drawing in and out. 'I...Oh, God, it feels good. It's been so long.'

I'm unsure what to make of her comment—it's been a long time since she's had a lover, or since she's touched herself? But

I don't care. Either way, I just want to see her come all over her fingers while I'm beside her.

'Show me,' I say.

Her eyes latch onto mine, confused.

'Show me how you make yourself come,' I say.

I can read the indecision in her eyes. I don't want a sexy show; I want her to touch herself like she does when no one's watching.

'I want to see you too.' She looks down my abs, to where my cock is straining against the shorts.

I nod, reaching for my waistband, then pause. Her eyes dart back up to mine. 'Don't come until I say,' I tell her. Then I pull my shorts down my hips until my cock is freely resting against my stomach. I take myself in my hand, stroking lightly. I growl out a curse. My cock is so hard and so sensitive it's not going to take me long. 'Now show me how you like it.'

She withdraws her fingers and parts her outer lips until that pleasure-seeking bundle of nerves is exposed, then she rubs herself in a circular motion. At the end of the bed, I see her toes curl.

Hell yeah.

Her breathing increases and grows ragged. I want it to be my fingers stroking her clit until she writhes and comes undone, but if it can't be me, then watching her do it is the next best thing.

Mia's chest is rising and falling fast, and her hips push upwards as her hand continues stroking. Her thighs fall open completely, treating me to a sight that makes my mouth water. Glistening pink flesh swollen with arousal. I want to sink inside her so bad, to memorize the way her hot cunt feels around me. But I won't. Not yet.

She watches me pull my cock in long, easy strokes. 'Are you imagining it's my hand on you?' she asks, slightly breathless.

'Fuck yeah,' I say, pumping my fist over the crown and groaning. 'But you'd be using two hands.' It's obvious to us both, given my generous size, and her delicate hands. 'And I'd make you go slow, so I could savor every bit of pleasure, the way your soft hands stroked my shaft while you were wishing it was your mouth.' Mia lets out a moan. 'I'd want to take my time, not come right away,' I admit.

Mia's fingers pick up speed as she circles the bud with a wet sound.

'I wish it was my tongue on your clit,' I say. 'I could spend hours fucking you with my mouth.'

She lets out a desperate whimper, and I know she's getting close. Her hips rock up with every stroke. I pump my cock harder.

'That's it. Come for me sweetheart, give me everything.'

She cries out, and her fingers still as she comes. I can see the muscles in her pussy tremble and imagine how incredible it would feel to have her clench around my cock. I come with a hoarse moan, spilling myself onto my chest and abs.

After, we lay side by side, watching each other as my pulse pounds in my ears. I'm desperate to take her in my arms, but I know I can't. She's not mine, even if we did just share an incredibly intimate moment. I might not have laid a finger on her, yet I feel closer to her than anyone. I want to apologize, to explain that we shouldn't have done that. But I'm not sorry. And I would do it again in a heartbeat.

We lay, unmoving, facing each other for several minutes. Mia searches my eyes for clues about what I'm thinking. 'Collins?' she asks, finally, her voice small.

I lean over her on the bed, petting her hair back away from her face. 'I'm sorry if I got a little carried away.'

She hesitates, and I wonder what she could be thinking. But then her expression lightens. 'This is better than the sleepovers we had when we were twelve.'

An unexpected laugh rumbles in my chest and I kiss her forehead. 'That was way fucking better. Are you okay?'

She nods. 'I'm great.'

'Good. I'm going to clean myself up quick.' I rise from the bed in search of something to clean myself off, but opt for a shower. I don't know what to think about the fact that I haven't been able to fuck my own girlfriend for weeks and I just came like a goddamn fire hose at my own hand with Mia beside me.

Ten minutes later, I emerge with a towel around my hips and see Mia lying in bed, dressed once again in her T-shirt.

'Let's get some sleep.' I pull on my discarded shorts from beside the bed and crawl beside her.

I have no idea how I'm going to be productive in meetings tomorrow with Pierre and his executives with the erotic image of Mia coming on her own fingers permanently tattooed into my brain.

I switch off the light and we lie silent in the dark a few moments before I feel the bed shift slightly, as Mia moves closer to me, releasing a sleepy sound. She curls her hand around mine and squeezes. 'Night, Coll,' she yawns.

'Goodnight, angel,' I murmur.

I lay awake for a long time after that as a rush of emotions charges through me without invitation. Part of me feels like shit for what I've done to Tatianna, yet the relief at knowing our relationship is over is immediate and all-encompassing, but most of all, I feel like I screwed up with Mia yet again.

Chapter Sixteen

Mia

Hand holding seems like the most juvenile thing I could have done after what Collins and I just shared. But I want to touch him—need to feel some part of him—because somehow that makes what I've just experienced more real.

My entire body is still singing from it. I've never pleasured myself in front of an audience before, and when Collins asked me to, I was so nervous, I wasn't sure what to do, but his rugged voice instructed me. As he growled out orders, and I did what he wanted, it was like he was doing it to me, and it was so much better than being alone. It was exciting, knowing that he was so turned on by watching me touch myself. The desperate hunger burning in his eyes ensured I would have done anything he'd asked.

And watching him tug his shorts down and free his cock tempted me beyond belief. Our first time, I remembered him being huge. He'd been so big back then, that even after the initial pain subsided, it had been hard to take him all the way in at first. And then he'd filled me so deep, so full. Still, when I thought back on it, I figured I'd only imagined his amazing size. But it really is huge. I figured my memories were only my imagination running wild, like one of my dad's fishing stories, he added inches to every retelling. But Collins is even bigger than I remembered.

Damn, his cock alone is reason enough to fly across the country on my last dime.

Watching him stroke himself, knowing that he was imagining me doing it to him, was so hot. It took every ounce of self-control for me to not touch him myself. I wanted to curl my hand around him and feel his thick length that I was sure would be hot to the touch.

But I knew he didn't want that. He wanted to do the right thing and wait until he'd finished things with Tatianna. I could see it in his eyes.

Even after. Especially after. He felt so guilty. And I hated seeing the guilt in his eyes. I hated that maybe I'd made him do something he wasn't ready to do yet. So I told him I was fine, and I was.

Mostly.

I don't remember falling asleep. I wake the next morning to the sun pouring into the hotel suite through its grand windows. My body feels relaxed and refreshed, like I've had the first good night's sleep since I lost my job. I stretch and turn to see Collins' side of the bed empty. I knew he was going to be in meetings with Pierre all day, but I was hoping I'd get to wish him luck before he left.

There's a note on the pillow next to me.

Mia,
    You looked so peaceful, I didn't want to wake you. I'm in meetings all day and part of the evening. Maybe we'll be able to get drinks tonight after dinner. Have fun seeing the city, but not too much.
    -C
    P.S. Text me if you get lost or need rescuing.

The offer of rescue brings a smile to my face. He's always there to rescue me if I need him.

My hand drifts over to Collins' empty side of the bed. I wish we could go out and see the city together, but I'll have to be my own company today.

I'm excited to explore Paris, so I shower and dress in no time. After devouring a flakey croissant and washing it down with rich coffee, I find myself spending most of the day in the Louvre. I hadn't planned on taking that much time, but the place is so vast that every time I think I've seen it all, there is another hallway, floor or building I have yet to explore. It's amazing, the number of master works in one place, the beauty of which nearly brings me to tears.

I save the Mona Lisa for last, and by the time I get there it's early evening. I have to wait in line for a bit, which gives me time to think. It really sinks in that I'm in Paris. Two weeks ago I was fired from a job for something I hadn't even done. A job where I was barely making my college loan payments, and struggling to make rent. I would never have dreamed I'd be here now, in Paris, and yet here I am in this beautiful city with my favorite person. I smile to myself, feeling a bit silly but also like the luckiest woman alive.

The line moves forward. I take a few steps closer. I'm almost to the front.

Collins is such an amazing man. And after last night, I'm pretty sure the only thing keeping us apart is his need to break it off with Tatianna. I hope so anyway. But what if last night was just a slip up for him? We never talked about it after. He never actually said he was going to end it with her. And I don't want to push him to break it off with her if that's not what he wants. Maybe I shouldn't have let last night happen. An uneasy feeling churns inside me.

The people in front of me move aside and I find myself in front of the Mona Lisa. I've seen prints of it so many times, still, when I step in front of the real painting, it takes my breath away. I can definitely see what all the hype is about. It's the subtlety of her expression that really gives me goosebumps. She's smiling as if she knows something I don't. I'm half tempted to ask her if she knows what I'm doing with Collins. Does she know if he wants to stay with Tatianna?

But Mona Lisa isn't talking, and a long line waits behind me to see her. So as my shoulders slump with these unanswered questions, I head to the exit and come out on the dimly lit streets. Collins said he wouldn't be back for dinner, so I decide to walk along the River Seine, hoping I'll find a good place to eat.

The city is bustling with tourists and Parisians alike, out enjoying the beautiful night. As I slowly make my way down the river, I notice everyone is in pairs. The couple in front of me is holding hands. On the boulevard, a man and woman sit on a park bench and look longingly into each other's eyes. I pass another couple leaning against the railing, gazing down on the river, arms around each other, huddling close.

Together.

As I take note of all the couples, my heart fills with sadness. I wrap my arms around myself, suddenly feeling cold, and alone. I've been wandering around this romantic city like a lovesick fool all day, but the man I've fallen for isn't even mine, and I'm not sure he ever will be.

The emptiness I feel is so sudden and so overwhelming it hurts, my eyes pool with tears.

At least two weeks ago I had a job and an apartment. Now, I have nothing. I want to believe Collins will leave Tatianna, but the cold truth is, I have no assurances.

I have no idea what comes next.

Chapter Seventeen

Collins

Another room opened up at the hotel, and I left Mia in the suite, in favor of a room to myself where I wouldn't have to share a bed with a woman who tempted me to my very core. I couldn't imagine spending the rest of the week fighting the urge to jump her each night. Especially since I knew she'd give in to me. She'd give me everything, if I only asked. It'd always been that way.

My meetings with Pierre and his associates went better than expected, so I should be returning on a high, but as Mia and I arrive home, feelings of sadness stir inside me.

Tatianna is in the kitchen when we arrive. She squeals and runs to me, throwing her arms around my neck dramatically, and I can't help but feel it's all for show, rather than a genuine display of affection.

'Missed you,' she says, air kissing my cheek.

I can't even muster the words back to her. My eyes follow Mia's movements. She turns away from us, but not before I catch a hint of sadness in her eyes. She heads to the fridge and grabs a bottle of water.

'Well, how was it? Paris, right?' she asks.

'How was New York?' I ask, my tone guarded.

She waves a dismissive hand, and I wonder if she's going to lie. 'Flaky photographer canceled. I stayed home.'

'You should have told me. You could have come with.' The words taste false in my mouth, and I know they're all wrong. Mia was the perfect companion. I just want to hear Tatianna admit that she wasn't the least bit concerned with me – she was out clubbing with God knows who.

She waves me off again. 'I'm sure Mia filled my role nicely.' She turns to Mia. 'Did you take care of my man?'

Mia's eyes widen and she nods. 'I did.' Her eyes find mine briefly, and then stray down to the floor.

Fuck. Mia isn't good at lying. She's just not that type of person. And now I feel like even more of an asshole because not only did I use her in Paris to fulfill my own needs, but now I've put her in a situation where she feels she has to lie.

'The trip went well,' I say, trying to smooth the awkward moment over.

Mia glances up again, her gaze finding Tatianna's. 'Collins was brilliant. He won over Pierre and Adele almost immediately.'

'You were amazing,' I correct her.

'Wait, who are Pierre and Adele?' Tatianna asks.

Mia's brows pinch together. 'Pierre Ducharme, the CEO of Ducharme Industries…the entire reason for the trip.' She seems shocked that Tatianna wouldn't know this information, since it was so important to me.

Tatianna nods. 'Oh. Right. So, was it all work or did you guys have some fun?'

Mia laughs nervously. 'We had fun. Collins made sure it was perfect for me.'

I bite down, my jaw clenching as memories of Mia's naked, curvy body dance through my brain, her moan of satisfaction when she tasted a real croque-monsieur for the first time, the mischievous twinkle in her eyes when she'd had too much wine, her hearty laugh when I took her to the top of the Eiffel Tower.

105

I exchange a meaningful look with Mia, as if to communicate my pleasure that she was the one with me. Tatianna's gaze moves between me and Mia and her brow furrows as if she's just solved a challenging equation. I see the exact moment something snaps in her. Her hands fly to her hips and her gaze narrows on Mia.

'What exactly has been going on here?' Tatianna questions Mia, her tone filled with icy venom.

Mia's mouth snaps shut, and she looks to me, desperate, her eyes wide and wild.

Not getting anything out of Mia, Tatianna turns to me. 'Have you been fucking her?' she shrieks.

I don't know what the fuck is wrong with me, but I don't answer right away. I just look at the woman I've spent the last three years with and wonder where all the time went. I feel like I've built more memories, shared more laughs, had more fun with Mia in one week than I have with Tatianna in three years.

Tatianna drops her head to look at the floor, and makes a sound of annoyed frustration. When she lifts her head, she's laughing. 'You're fucking crazy to choose *that* over this.' She motions between her and Mia—noting the obvious differences in their physiques. Tatianna is tall and willowy, while Mia is curvy and built for a man's pleasure.

'I haven't been fucking her, as you so delicately put it. But Mia and I…' I pause and draw a breath, searching for the right words. 'We need to talk, Tatianna.'

'Oh, hell no,' Tatianna roars. 'How dare you choose this chubby, plain loser over me?' She spits the words like an accusation.

Mia shrinks back toward the wall, hugging her arms around herself and her eyes fill with tears. I step between the two women. 'Stop,' I say, my voice cutting off Tatianna's. I place my hand on Mia's cheek and she leans into my touch. I want to tell her it will all be okay, but I let my hand fall away, then I face Tatianna. 'No one speaks to Mia that way.' I can't help but draw a parallel between this moment and the first day I met Mia. I stood up for her then too. It turns out, it's instinctual for me. I won't let anyone hurt her.

'It's over, Tatianna. We're done. I want you gone by tonight.'

'You're a fucking asshole,' she says.

'That may be, but we both know this relationship isn't going anywhere. It isn't leading toward anything. It's time for us to move on.'

'Sorry, but I'll never be a soccer mom if that's what you're looking for. I thought we were on the same page,' she barks.

I shake my head, unwilling to answer. I don't want to argue the finer points of our differences in front of Mia. It won't accomplish anything, and I won't change my mind. 'I'll have my assistant arrange for a moving company.'

'And where exactly am I supposed to go?' she asks.

Ah, there it is, the real reason she's stayed with me all this time. I've provided her with a beautiful home, and extravagant lifestyle she could never afford on her own.

I want to tell her maybe the man she was with last Friday night will take care of her, but I know that tossing out that accusation won't make any of this better. 'I guess you have some things to figure out in the next few hours,' I say, instead.

She grabs her purse from the counter and storms past us, causing Mia to squeak in surprise.

Chapter Eighteen

Mia

My jetlagged brain struggles to comprehend what just happened.

I can't seem to wrap my tired brain around it.

Tatianna's words were sharp and hateful, her venom directed at me. Maybe I deserved it. Hadn't I just stormed into their life and pulled them apart? But I don't have that kind of power. I can't make people do anything they don't want to do.

Certainly no one can make Collins do anything he doesn't want to do.

Still, I'm having a hard time understanding what just happened. Did he really just break up with Tatianna? Right in front of me?

Tatianna storms past me, her face filled with so much anger a small shriek escapes me, and I flinch.

Her heels click down the hall and rush up the steps. Somewhere above a door slams.

My eyes are fixed to the floor. I want to look at Collins. I want to know if he's okay, but I'm scared to look up. I'm scared he'll be mad at me for coming in here and ruining his perfect life with his supermodel girlfriend.

I'm such a jerk. Why did I come?

I expect Collins to storm out after her, or to curse me out, or something. Instead he remains a few feet away, leaning against the counter. When I finally find the courage to look up at his face he has his phone out. His features are relaxed and don't give anything away. He taps out a message on his phone. He must be arranging for the movers or something.

I silently watch him, hoping I haven't completely ruined our friendship by showing up here and messing with his life. Finally, he looks up and sees that I'm still huddled against the wall. Stuffing his phone into his pocket, Collins stalks over to me.

'I'm sorry you had to see that,' he grumbles. His low voice makes me feel even worse.

'It's okay.' My own voice comes out shaky and quiet. 'Are you all right?'

Dark eyes, deep with emotion latch onto mine, and he nods. 'Yes.'

He sounds confident, but his eyes and the expression on his face leave me feeling unsure. He's so guarded and serious. I hate it.

When have I ever felt so unsure around Collins?

Never.

He places his palm against my cheek. 'I'm sorry you had to deal with that,' he says softly.

'Don't worry about it. I don't mind.' I didn't like what Tatianna said, but to know that he's finally free of that controlling woman who is all wrong for him? I'd go through that again in a heartbeat.

I have no idea what happens next, and I'm afraid to ask. I chew on my lip, listening to the sound of heels click around upstairs and doors slam. Collins drops his hand away, but he continues hovering over me, watching me like he's waiting to see if I really am okay.

'Do you think it's okay if I go upstairs and shower?' I ask. I'm jetlagged and grubby from the long flight. Plus I can't help but think Collins must need to be alone right now to process what just went down.

'Of course.' He nods.

I head toward the stairs, feeling Collins' eyes on me the entire time.

The shower is hot and the water soothing as I wash away the grime from the long flight. But it can't wash away the guilt I have over coming here in the first place. Collins was always so good at saving me. It's no wonder that, when I lost my job and had nowhere else to turn, I ran to him. Because if anyone could fix my failing life it was him. But is it fair of me to burden him with my issues? Is it fair of me to expect him to stop everything and rescue me from my pathetic fate? Is it fair of me to hope he'll drop everything he's been working for his whole life to build, just to save me?

The answer is so obvious. Hell no. As the hot water pelts my back I search for a way I can make this right, but I can't. I've come in here, messed things up, and now the only thing to do is to leave him alone so that he has time to heal.

I get out of the shower and dry myself off, dressing in a T-shirt. I climb in bed and am just about to turn the light out when my phone rings. It's Leila.

'Hey,' I answer flatly.

'Mia,' her voice is concerned. 'What's wrong?' She can read me like a book.

'I think it might be time for me to go home. Is that offer for your couch still open?' I ask.

'Of course it is, but what happened?'

'Collins just broke up with her,' I say.

Leila is quiet for a second as if she is trying to understand what I just said. Finally she says, 'I don't get it. If he's single now, isn't that what you wanted?'

She's right. It *was* what I wanted, but now that it's happened, I'm not sure it's right. I don't think it's what I want now. 'He's upset. I feel like I've screwed up his life by coming here.'

'No,' she says. 'You're over thinking this. You always over think things. You care about him. He cares about you. Just give him some time and space. Breakups are hard.'

I'm not sure it's the right thing to do, and I tell her this, but Leila is insistent. In the end she talks me into staying a little longer.

Maybe I can help him out somehow. Offer my support, for what it's worth.

Over the next two days, I give Collins space, spending the bulk of my time applying for more jobs. He isn't around much anyway, and when he is, he seems to be hard at work, so I don't bother him. I've gotten to the point where I think there really is no reason for me to be here, since we never see each other anyway, when he comes in the kitchen one morning with a smile on his face. The first smile I've seen on him in days. I can't help but feel encouraged and excited by the light in his eyes.

'Good news,' he says. He pulls a stack of papers out from behind his back and places them in front of me with a flourish.

'What is this, your memoirs?' I ask. The stack is thick.

He shakes his head. 'It's a power of attorney, an agreement, and supporting documents from the investigation of your termination.'

'I'm sorry, it's what?' It's not that I don't understand the words he's using, I just have no idea how they fit together to make any sense, at all. 'An agreement to what?'

'I had your boss investigated. They found the proof my attorneys needed to negotiate a settlement for you. They'll pay you one hundred thousand dollars and agreed to hire you back.'

'You had my boss investigated?' I take a sip of my morning coffee in the hopes it will help me understand everything Collins is springing on me.

'I wanted it to be a surprise, so I had them draw everything up. All they need from you is a signature on the limited power of attorney so they can finish the deal on your behalf.'

Collins looks so happy, yet my face is turning red, and tears pool in my eyes. He negotiated it so that I would get my old job back. I swallow against the huge lump forming in my throat. I want to be happy. God how I want to, because he's doing it again. He's saving me from my stupid employment bungle. I should be thanking him. I should take my job back. He's gotten me a great deal.

But it's not what I want. I don't want to move back to Connecticut. I want to be here with him. And more important than that, I want him to want me here, too.

But I guess he doesn't. I really am a burden to him. One he's willing to put the time and money into sending far, far away.

I wipe shakily at a tear streaming down my face. 'I'm sorry, Collins.'

He tilts my chin up and meets my eyes. 'Why are you sorry?'

'I shouldn't have come,' I murmur, wiping at another stray tear that's escaped.

'Why not?' His tone is whisper soft, and his expression is full of concern and tenderness.

'Because,' I manage, sucking in a breath, 'I charged into your perfect life and ruined everything for you and Tatianna. It's not your job to rescue me.'

Bringing both hands to my face, his warm palms cup my cheeks and he wipes away the last of my tears. 'You haven't ruined anything. Come sit down and let me explain some things to you.'

'Okay,' I agree, my heart aching and my head spinning with unanswered questions.

Chapter Nineteen

Collins

I guide Mia into the adjoining family room, my fingertips at her lower back. I have no idea what caused her to break down, and I don't handle crying females very well. I never have. Maybe it's the result of growing up with two brothers. Maybe it's the result of being with Tatianna, who rarely showed her emotions.

We sit down on the sofa, and she curls her legs underneath her on the cushion, bracing for whatever I'm about to tell her.

I huff out a sigh and contemplate how to begin. 'You didn't ruin anything between me and Tatianna. Things had been deteriorating for a long time.' I don't tell her that I'd lost my ability to orgasm with her or that I hated the lack of concern and interest she showed in my life. 'The breakup was overdue. You being here might have actually prolonged it.'

'What?' She blinks at me, waiting for me to continue. She assumed that her presence sped up my demise with Tatianna when in fact it was the opposite.

'When you showed up here, a thousand emotions I hadn't felt in fifteen years raced through me. Emotions I didn't have time for, or frankly want to feel. My life was easy. My company was my focus, and I had my brothers to lean on for support. Tatianna was…' *Shit, this is going to sound harsh.* 'She was here for my physical pleasure.'

Mia flinches like someone backhanded her.

I reach for her hand and she lets me take it, but it's limp and lifeless in my own.

'These last several weeks even that wasn't working between us,' I admit.

Her eyebrows pinch together. 'What do you mean?'

'I haven't slept with Tatianna since you arrived. And even before that, I'm embarrassed to say… Well, let's just say, my body knew something my head didn't.'

'Okay…' She draws out the word, her eyes searching mine for understanding.

I'm not making any sense, and I know that. I take a deep breath and prepare to start over.

'Then why did you stay with her?' Mia interrupts.

'If I was single, I'd have no excuse not to pursue you. The idea of you and I both single and under one roof scared me.'

She chews on her lip, looking unsure. 'So, you don't want me here. I get it, Coll. I'll take my old job and move on.'

Shaking my head, I tug her hand into my lap and grip my fingers between hers, like that will somehow show her how I feel. 'Let me finish.'

She waits, watching me, hardly breathing while I search for the right words.

'When you showed up here and reminded me of a promise I made when I was ten years old, it scared the shit out of me. I used my relationship, as damaged as it was, as a buffer to avoid my real feelings. But I can't do that any longer. I have no idea what the future holds, and I need to take this one day at a time, but I want more.'

'More?' she asks, her tone guarded.

'Yes. More. I don't know what that means, and I can't have this marriage promise hanging over our heads. We're friends first. And whatever happens between us, I'm not willing to lose you as a friend. I need you to understand that before things go any further.'

'I understand.' She takes a moment, her eyes wide, watching me. 'So you don't want me to leave?' she asks, her voice small.

'Of course not,' I say. There is so much unexplored sexual tension between us, but more than that, there are real feelings too. A strange feeling comes over me and my chest tightens. It matters to her how I feel, if I'm eating, if I'm happy. It's kind of like how my brothers understand me, even when I'm barely stringing two words together. Mia just gets me. The real me. I know I don't deserve her tenderness, the concern she's shown me the last few days as my ex moved out and I threw myself into my work. I had a girlfriend I'd been stringing along, all because I was scared of my future with Mia. She's a forever kind of girl. And after my mom died, I didn't want to give my heart to another woman. But the thing about Mia is that she had it already. She's had it all along.

'But why did you get me my old job back?' she asks.

'Because it didn't sit right with me knowing that your name had been tarnished. Because you spend all your free time looking for a job, and whenever you talk about your past, your face gets this pouty expression. I wanted you to have choices. Not to be stuck here, living with me by default. That's what Tatianna did... I'm not looking to be anyone's second choice.'

'You could never be my second choice,' she whispers. 'You were my first everything.'

I give her hand a squeeze. Regret over the night I took her virginity still churns inside of me but I push it aside. 'Are we okay?' I ask.

She nods. 'Yes, but what happens next?'

'That depends. If you go back home to your old job, we keep in touch and visit as often as we can. And if you stay here...we have a lot of catching up to do from the past fifteen years.'

'If you're sure you're okay with it, we do have a lot of catching up to do…'

We're both quiet as the meaning behind this moment sinks in. Mia is moving in with me. Tatianna is gone and all but forgotten.

'Are you pissed at me about how I handled things with Tatianna?' I ask.

'No,' she says, without hesitation. 'I think it had to happen that way. We both needed time.'

I nod. 'I still think about that night, you know.'

Her eyes, bright with desire, dance on mine. She knows exactly which night I'm referring to. 'I do too.'

'I still feel like an asshole,' I admit.

'What? Why?' she asks, like she genuinely doesn't know.

'I saw the blood smears on your inner thighs. I know I hurt you. I didn't know what I was doing and … I still hate that you didn't get off.' The weight of my admission presses down on my shoulders. It's been buried inside me all this time and it feels good to finally talk about this.

'You didn't hurt me.' She shakes her head. 'Well, I mean, you did, but not on purpose. Your size was….well…' She becomes flustered and clamps her mouth shut. She takes a deep breath, then she starts again. 'You were so tender. It was exactly what I wanted, please don't feel bad about it. You were sweet and careful. I remember it perfectly. Don't ruin it for me.'

'You remember it quite differently then,' I manage. My throat feels tight as I watch her.

'I remember the weight of your body on mine and how you stole my breath when you first entered me, and then how we found our rhythm and moved together. And how it lasted longer than I thought it would.'

My chest swells with pride. That surprised me too. I remember thinking it'd be over in about a minute, but then I was so worried about her, and over thinking everything that it distracted me from the immense pleasure threatening to overwhelm me.

'Come here.' I pull her close and she curls her body into mine, letting me hold her. She looks beautiful, even with her tear-stained cheeks and pink nose. I hold her the way I should have done that night so long ago. The warm weight of her against my side eases some of my guilt.

I want to hold her in my lap and kiss her, but I don't want to rush her. Something tells me neither of us would need much convincing to take this upstairs and tear each other's clothes off. And considering the sheets I shared with another woman are still on my bed, it wouldn't be right.

Unable to resist the temptation of her warm body pressing against mine, I tilt her chin, angling her mouth just right, then I lean down and kiss her. It's an innocent kiss, my lips touching hers just lightly, tasting her sweetness. But it's a kiss that holds the promise of more to come. And even though we kiss until we're out of breath, it ends much too soon.

When we part, she stays glued to my side, one arm flung around my middle, like she's unwilling to let me go.

'Did you say one hundred thousand dollars?' she asks, her mouth curling into a silly grin.

I chuckle, despite the intensity of the mood. 'I did. And you deserve every cent for the way they dragged your name through the mud and booted you out without a proper investigation.'

'Thank you for always being my hero,' she says.

'Thank you for always being my gremlin.' I smile at her and she smacks me in the arm.

'Can't believe you still call me that stupid nickname.'

'Speaking of the Gremlin, tomorrow is Sunday. I invited the whole crew to join us on the yacht if you're up for it.'

'Of course,' she says. 'I would love to.'

*

It felt good to clear the air last night between me and Mia. Better than I could have imagined, actually. So today, I'm relaxed and happy as we board the Gremlin. Pace carries Max around the boat, showing him every gadget and knob while Kylie watches them lovingly. Colton and Sophie arrive next and stroll over to where Mia and I are standing beside the railing, looking at the water.

'Mia! It's so good to see you,' Sophie says, pulling her in for a hug.

Colton's eyes meet mine, and he seems to understand that Tatianna is gone for good. 'Good fucking call, bro,' he says, thumping me on the back. He and Sophie rarely joined us on the yacht when it was just Tatianna and I. He didn't enjoy her company, and I can't say I blamed him. Now that I'm free of her, I just feel better. More lighthearted than I have in years. It's strange what being in Mia's presence does for me.

'Pace and Kylie are here, I think just below deck showing everything to Max,' I say.

Colton nods. 'Good. When they get back, we have an announcement to make.' He pulls Sophie close and they share a secret smile.

I have a feeling I know what the announcement is going to be. They were just married about six weeks ago, and I'm quite certain they fuck like rabbits.

When Pace emerges from downstairs, Colton waves them over. Then he takes Sophie's hand, interlacing their fingers. 'Do you want to tell them, or should I?' he asks, softly. I've never seen him quite so soft and tender. A feeling of warmth washes over me.

'We're pregnant!' Sophie squeals, like she can't contain the secret even a second longer.

'Ah!' Kylie cries out, lunging for Sophie as she hugs her tightly. Mia's smile is wide and she bounces up and down, as if waiting for her turn to hug the mother-to-be.

'Nice job, dude,' Pace says, clapping Colton on the back.

'Congratulations,' I tell him, shaking his hand.

'Thanks guys. We're pretty excited,' Colton says, pulling Sophie into his arms and kissing her. 'She's just six weeks along, so it's still early, but we're over the moon.'

Pace tosses Max up in the air and tells him he's going to get a baby cousin.

The mood is happy and light, and I'm immensely pleased that my brothers have found so much happiness. The women take Max and retreat to the bow where there are scattered cushions for sunbathing. They talk excitedly, asking Sophie how she's been feeling and when her due date is.

My brothers and I settle in the deck chairs overlooking the ocean. And even though it's early, when James brings by a tray of frozen mojitos, we each accept one. There is a lot to celebrate today. Colton requests a virgin drink be sent over to his wife. I smile, knowing he uses any excuse he can to refer to her as his wife.

We sip our drinks as the yacht cuts effortlessly through the water.

'So, how are things going with Mia now that Tatianna's out of the picture?' Colton asks.

I glance over at Mia who has stripped out of her clothes and is making a turquoise bikini her bitch. *Goddamn.* A warm shudder flutters through me. 'Good,' I mumble.

Pace laughs. 'You've got to give us more than that, old man. Are you guys together or what?'

'I'm working on it.' I'm not sure what else to say. My brain tells me I should go slow, explore where this could lead, while my body screams at me to make her mine. Visions of her on her hands and knees while I pump into her from behind make my vision cloud with lust. I don't know how much longer I can hold back. I want to know how things could be between us now that we're both all grown up. I drop a pillow into my lap in an attempt to conceal the half-erection I struggle to fight off.

Pace laughs. 'Still haven't fucked her.'

'Shut the fuck up unless you want to be tossed overboard,' I warn, my tone coming out harsh and ruthless. But goddamn, being this close to Mia for the past several weeks, she's completely gotten under my skin.

My eyes wander over to her again. She's gently touching Sophie's belly and while there's nothing to suggest she's pregnant, Mia looks at her in complete awe. It's beautiful. I can't help watching Mia as she plays with Max, tickling his belly, and playing a silly game with him using her sunglasses. I'm awestruck, unable to look away. She will make a beautiful mother, and I feel overcome with emotion.

I listen to my brothers tease me, telling me they're both fathers now, and it's my turn next, but my attention stays captured by Mia. She is beautiful in so many ways.

'Excuse me, guys,' I say, pushing out of my chair and heading purposely toward Mia.

When I reach her, I extend my hand, and she takes it without question and rises to her feet.

'Collins?' she asks, letting me lead her below deck. I get the sense she'd let me do just about anything right now.

I don't respond just yet, because I'm afraid of what I might say, instead I continue guiding her into one of the cabins.

'What are you…'

'Do you trust me?' I ask closing and locking the bedroom door behind us.

'Yes,' she says without hesitation.

I turn and face her, my body pressing her up against the back of the door. A primal growl eases up my throat as my mouth ghosts over hers. 'I'm scared of all of this. My feelings for you, what the future holds, all of it. But I know one thing.'

'What?' she asks, her chest rising with an inhale while her lips brush mine.

'I need you,' I whisper.

Her eyes implore mine for several seconds, trying to figure out what exactly it is I need.

When my hands settle against her hips and my fingers sink into the edges of her bikini bottoms, it becomes abundantly clear. 'Are you okay with this?' I ask, giving her a chance to pull away.

'I need you too,' she admits.

My heart jumps at her admission. I untie the strings at her hips, and her bikini bottoms fall to the floor. Mia watches me closely, instantly grasping that I'm no longer the nervous fumbling teenage boy from her memories. As far as I'm concerned, this is our real first time. A chance for me to redeem myself and make this good for her.

I reach between us, lightly rubbing one finger over her smooth sex. A murmur rises up her throat and I feel her grow wet. I've barely touched her, but she's so responsive.

She's much more confident with her body than I remember, pushing her hips into my hands and moaning when my fingertip makes contact with her clit. I kiss her deeply, and her tongue strokes mine while I work her over. *Hell yeah.*

She reaches behind her neck and unties the strings holding her top in place. Loving how bold she is, I toss the fabric away, wanting her completely bare.

Her body rocks against my hand as she unlaces my shorts and pushes her hand inside. I feel her hand curl around me, and she gasps.

'I love how big you are,' she says. Hot pride rips through me. While Mia strokes my cock, I push one finger inside her. Watching her do this to herself while under my command in Paris has fueled my fantasies every day since. Her body grips me and makes a wet sucking sound each time I pump my fingers in and out.

'You're so wet for me,' I whisper against her lips.

'Yes, only you, Collins, only you.'

I think I understand what she's telling me. *I* get her this way. This turned on and wanting. 'You still have the tightest pussy I've ever felt,' I growl into the side of her neck. I want to be inside her, but I refuse to rush through foreplay like I did the first and last time I fucked her.

She moans and tilts her pelvis closer. I recognize her throaty cries signal that she's close to orgasm already.

'That's it, ride it out,' I whisper. Lowering my mouth to her breasts, I treat them to wet kisses, sucking on her nipples and flicking my tongue across their firm peaks.

Mia shatters, moaning out my name as she comes.

Her body trembles when I remove my fingers and she sways on her feet. Her movements still and my body mourns the loss of her touch.

'Come here, I've got you.' I guide her over onto the bed, and once she's settled, I shove my shorts to the floor. Joining her in the center of the mattress, I pull her close. It should feel strange that I'm in bed with a very naked Mia— my friend—but it's the most natural thing in the world.

Lifting her chin to mine, I kiss her deeply. I hope she understands that I've only just begun exploring her body. There's so much more I want to do. Kissing my way from her lips, to her neck, to her breasts, she giggles when I reach her belly.

'Ticklish?' I ask.

She grins down at me. 'You know I am.'

She's right. I know she's ticklish on her stomach and under her arms, and I know she's honest and kind and has the biggest damn heart of anyone I've ever met. And I know I wouldn't trade this moment with her for anything in the world.

'Open for me,' I tell her, moving one of her legs so it's draped over my shoulder.

'Collins,' she whines.

'Don't get shy on me now,' I tease. I kiss along her inner thighs, moving from one to the next. 'After that night in Paris, I need to taste you.'

She opens for me, her legs spread wide, and I lick her from the top to the bottom until my tongue finds her swollen clit. She whimpers. 'Does that feel good?' I ask.

'Yeah,' she manages to gasp.

She runs her fingers through my hair, pressing into me. The only thing that matters is her pleasure, and I throw myself into it fully, sucking and running my tongue over her hot flesh in a pace that quickens as my need to be inside her intensifies. I don't stop until she's crying out my name and desperately clinging to my shoulders as she comes apart.

As the spasms slow, and I pull away, her warm eyes refuse to break from mine as I crawl up her body, kissing her neck, her face, her eyelids, and any part of her I can find.

'That's two,' I say. 'Think you can handle one more?'

She blinks at me, seemingly surprised that I've been counting her orgasms. Her eyes are glazed over with lust. 'I—I don't know,' she admits.

I chuckle darkly, and stroke her body, running my hands along her smooth skin, lifting her ass to cup in my hands. When I press into her, stimulating her core, a gasp escapes. 'That's what you're doing to me, Mia,' I growl near her ear. 'Is this something you're ready to deal with?'

Unable to speak, she nods as a low moan escapes her lips.

I'm rock hard and ready when all my wicked plans grind to an excruciating halt. I don't have a condom. Mia shakes her head, tells me it's okay. I can only assume that she means she's on birth control and trusts that I'm disease-free, which I am, but her complete faith in me is astounding. Running my fingers through the long strands of her hair, I watch her eyes, trying to make certain she's sure. There will be no going back after this, and as much as I hate that I'm rushing it, we've spent years building to this exact moment.

With her laying on her back, I kneel before her and angle myself to her center. Her eyes drift closed. 'Open them for me,' I say. She opens her eyes and they are dark with her desire. 'Keep them open. I want you to watch us. I want you to know it's me inside you.'

She grunts as I inch forward and meet resistance. I can already tell that my memories of her fitting around me like a hot glove were not overblown. She's perfect. I feed her my cock, one inch at a time, working myself slowly inside her so she can adjust. She wiggles against the bed and claws at the sheets. But true to my order, her eyes drift between mine and to where our bodies are joined.

'That's it. Can you take more of me?' I want to pound home hard and fast, but I won't move until she tells me it's okay.

'Please, Collins. I want all of you,' she begs.

I press forward as far as I can go and grind against her, stimulating her clit with my length buried fully within. Her breath catches in her throat. There are five painful seconds where I know she can't breathe, and I watch in agony as she struggles to catch her breath, her mouth open, but her chest still. 'Breathe baby.' I lean down and whisper against her lips, withdrawing just a fraction. Her mouth opens and she sucks in air. One shaky breath, and then another. And then she's clawing her nails down my back, winding her legs around my waist, and she's writhing against me like she can't get enough.

Fuck.

Unable to hold back any longer, I set a rhythm, sliding in and out of her warmth. She is mind-blowingly amazing, and I know I won't ever recover from this, as long as I live. With a loud gasp and her fingers in my hair, Mia comes again. I soon follow, groaning out her name with my face buried against the soft skin of her neck.

Chapter Twenty

Mia

I can't say how many times I imagined what it would be like if I ever had sex with Collins again. Countless times, each one was a tribute to my memories of our first time, and to how practiced and sure he would be the next time we were together. Each time I imagined being with him, it was incredible.

Yet none of those times can hold a candle to the way it actually played out. He was so attentive, so amazingly responsive to my bodies every need. I know in an instant, he's ruined me for all other men.

I will never forget that when he came he buried his face against my neck and groaned out my name. That sound on his lips, in his rough voice, breathed against my skin was one of the best moments of my life. And now, his strong arms hold me close, as my body trembles in his arms.

'Are you cold?' he asks.

I shake my head and look up at him embarrassed. 'My body is still...' I suppress a smile.

He chuckles, kissing me on the forehead, then pulls me closer against his hot bare chest.

Our first time together had been wonderful, a memory I will forever hold close to my heart. But that first time, just after, I rushed to dress, self-conscious that I'd just seduced my best friend and fled for home, with the excuse that I needed to help my family pack for the move the next day. We hadn't held each other afterwards and had no time to talk about how it felt.

Here we are, fifteen years later, and now we finally have that chance to hold each other. It feels so right, being here in his strong arms. I know I'm the luckiest woman alive, because in Collins I have the best of both worlds. He's my closest friend, and now my lover. He knows me better than anyone—inside and out.

'Three.' I say and smile at him through half closed eyes.

'Three times,' he grumbles and smiles back. He knows exactly what I'm counting. 'I owed you one or two, for the time back on my father's boat.' He dips down and kisses me gently on the lips.

I kiss him back. 'You don't owe me anything. I told you, that night was perfect.'

A relaxed smile spreads across his face and fills me with joy. 'This is perfect too.'

As I lie in his arms, we talk together about old times, between stealing kisses. He brushes my hair back from my face so gently, I can feel his concern for me in every movement, every tender gesture.

'Thank you for coming out with us on the boat today. It means a lot that you're here spending time with my family.'

I giggle. 'I wouldn't call what we're doing right now 'spending time with your family,'' I say, drawing a line down his firm chest with my finger. I'm tempted to bring my hand down lower, and see if I can entice him for more. But I feel a pang of guilt and stop my hand short, instead saying, 'Speaking of your family, maybe we should go back out there and rejoin the group. You being the *host* and all.' Thank God he has a captain to drive the boat.

I can tell he's not ready to end our time alone, neither am I, but he sees reason. 'Fine, let's get cleaned up.' He growls as he sits up, and pulls me into his arms. I squeal and wrap my arms around his neck as he carries me into the bathroom.

In the shower we lather the soap together and first he helps me clean off, his rough hands slip smoothly over my back, my arms, my hips. I savor every touch from him, and his hands relish my body's every curve. Next I help him clean up. My hands slide along his smooth muscular body, appreciating his hard muscles. His six-pack abs are too much for me to resist and I run my fingers down his stomach.

He pulls back laughing.

'Sorry,' I say. 'I forgot you're ticklish, too.'

He quickly pulls me back to him. 'You don't ever need to apologize for touching me,' he says. He reaches behind me and turns the water off, then reaches out and grabs a towel, wrapping it around me.

As we get dressed, there is a knock on the door. 'You guys got it out of your system yet?' It's Pace.

Collins' eyes darken, and I can see in his reaction that Pace has just broken some guy code, but then Collins meets my eyes and his expression softens once again.

Collins tugs his shorts back on, and checks to make sure I'm covered by my bikini before he answers the door. 'This isn't Dad's small boat, plenty of other bedrooms to choose from.' His voice drops at the last word as if he's not seeing who he'd expected beyond the open door. I peak around him and find Pace holding Max's hand and giggle.

'Hey, little guy,' Collins turns to Max. 'What's up?'

'Max and I were exploring and found the theater room. He was wondering if we could watch a movie. We tried to figure it out without you, but we can't seem to find the remote, and nothing works without that thing.'

'Of course we can watch a movie,' Collins says. He slips his hand around mine, and we all head to the theater to find everyone else already in there. Sophie and Colton have claimed one of the four love seats, Kylie is sitting on another, and Max runs over to join her.

'What movie should we watch?' Collins asks as he pulls the remote out of a hidden panel in the wall. We take one of the unclaimed seats and he wraps his arm around me. I curl up against his side.

'Gremlins!' Max shouts. I realize it's an odd request right away. I was born the year the movie came out, and only know about it because of my old thrift store shirt, the one I wore the first time Collins saved me.

Sophie giggles, 'What's Gremlins?'

Kylie turns back to her, 'It's the movie Collins named his boat after.'

Pace laugh-snorts. 'Yeah, that's right, Collins named his boat after an eighties movie.' His voice drips with sarcasm.

Colton joins him laughing. 'Yeah, he just can't get enough of those cute furry creatures.'

Sophie jabs Colton in the side. 'What? What's so funny?'

Pace is laughing so hard he can't answer, but Colton finally manages. 'He named his boat after his first love.' His voice is teasing.

Sophie and Kylie look at the guys as if they're nuts.

I feel my cheeks flush and attempt to hide my face in Collins' chest.

'Gremlin is his nickname for Mia,' Colton finishes.

'Awe,' Sophie and Kylie both sing out at the same time. Their eyes are full of envy.

I give them both a meek grin. Then look up at Collins, expecting him to be angry at his brothers for breaking the guy code again. I'm surprised to find his eyes, kind and caring, staring lovingly back into mine. He chuckles and kisses the top of my head. Apparently, he's totally okay with this round of jabs. And more than that, he's not denying it. He's not even embarrassed by his brothers calling me his first love. My heartbeat kicks up, and I reach up and kiss him.

'Ugh,' Pace says. 'Get a room.'

The others laugh. Then he thinks better of it. 'Never mind. We'd never see you again. Stay, but let's keep things PG.' He squeezes into the loveseat next to Max and Kylie, throwing his arm around Max as if to emphasize why we are keeping things PG.

Collins says, 'Right, Gremlins.' He pulls out the remote and locates the movie easily on one of his satellite services.

'You've seen this, right?' he asks me.

I shake my head.

'You mean all this time you just let me call you gremlin, and you weren't even curious?'

'I knew from the shirt it's a cute little fuzzy creature.'

Collins shakes his head incredulously and sets the movie to play. He dims the lights, and I settle in next to him. The others all settle in too. I look around me, feeling warmed by their company. I know that we haven't talked seriously about our future, but still, being here with him, and with his family, everything just feels right. I wonder, and hope that gatherings like this one might become a tradition. I'd love to be able to look forward to family day on the boat each Sunday.

I realize that when I showed up here several weeks ago I was ashamed and embarrassed by my situation and am happy to find that is no longer the case. Now I know I've got nothing to be ashamed of. I feel wanted. And I love it.

Collins leans down and whispers that we should stay the night on the boat and I gaze up at him, my heart filled to bursting.

Chapter Twenty-One

Collins

I power down my laptop, and gather up my belongings from my desk. It's Friday, time to start the weekend, and can't wait to spend it with Mia. Dating Mia Monroe is an experience I was wholly unprepared for. She's fun and carefree and easy going. Nothing like the Botoxed, uptight women I've been with since moving to LA.

Mia and I have been casually dating for the past two weeks. We've been to the ballet, made a trip to a world-renowned winery, and attended a designer's first showing of a jewelry collection— during which, Mia actually yawned. It's time to change up my game. This is *Mia. My Mia.* And tonight I've got something perfect planned. At least I hope I do.

Smiling to myself as I stroll toward the elevator, I say goodbye to a few dedicated employees who are still here after five o'clock on a Friday. There was an office-poll about my recent transformation. Apparently I look more rested, smile more often, and just seem happier. Shit, one brave soul even asked if I'd had work done, implying I'd gotten plastic surgery. They thought I was unaware of the whispering and quiet conversations had behind cubicle walls. But I wasn't. In fact I was as curious about this transformation as they were. At first, they assumed my twenty-three-year-old supermodel girlfriend was responsible for the smile on my face.

But then they'd seen Mia bring me lunch one day—a steak sandwich from my favorite deli—and realized I was no longer dating Tatianna. I didn't say a word. I actually thought the whole thing was quite humorous. Besides, it was none of their damn business. I felt happy and ten years younger, and it wasn't just the fantastic sex I was having. It was because Mia brought out the best in me. I grin as I pass by a particularly chatty administrative assistant. Raising one eyebrow, her gaze darts away from mine and she begins frantically typing on her keyboard. I have a feeling if I look closer, it'll all be gibberish. 'Good night, Miss Corrigan,' I say.

'Good night, sir,' she squeaks.

Chuckling to myself, I punch the button for the elevator that will take me to the underground parking garage. Picturing how the night's events will go, I can't help the satisfied grin that uncurls on my mouth. Mia is going to be beside herself when she sees what I have planned.

It's also the night I'm going to tell her that I want her to officially move in with me—not just crash in a guest room with her things tucked away in a suitcase that she could tow away at a moment's notice, but to move into my bedroom with me. Share my home with me. I'm excited as shit, and I know if I admitted any of this to my brothers, they'd accuse me of growing a vagina. But things beneath my trousers have never been better. In fact, I felt like a teenager again, growing hard at the mere thought of Mia—often at inopportune times, like in a staff meeting. I pull out my cell and text her.

I have something fun planned tonight. Dress casual.

She replies just as I'm settling into my car.

I can't wait to see you. I'm leaving work now.

She's begun working at a big law firm downtown in their accounting department, and she says she loves it. As long as she's happy. Mia has taught me so much, most of which is that life is too damn short to spend it being unhappy.

After she fell asleep in my bed last night, I grabbed *The Gremlin Files* and sat with her old scrapbook in my lap, pouring through every photograph, and every doodled word. The pages were crinkled and worn and her soft, feminine scent clung to them. There was a picture of me and Mia, from years ago. She was missing her two front teeth, but smiling as big as she could at the camera. I was looking at her. The look on my face was pure joy. I stared at that picture for the longest time. I felt like that boy again, like I'd recaptured some special piece of my youth. A memory I hadn't thought of in many years drifted into my head. It was my ninth birthday party, and after my mother sliced my birthday cake, I passed the biggest slice to Mia. My mother leaned over and kissed my cheek, and said, 'you're going to marry that girl someday.' Emotion like I hadn't felt in years crawled up my throat, lodging a hard lump there. I'd closed the book and wandered back to bed with Mia, curling my body around hers, with a feeling I couldn't describe for the life of me. Raw emotions over losing my mother were fresh in my mind as were my growing feelings for the woman in my arms. I awoke with a greater sense of purpose and clarity than I'd ever felt.

'Just tell me where we're going,' Mia says, bouncing in her seat.

I glance over at her briefly, before returning my eyes to road. 'Patience, little one.' I pat the top of her head.

I'd pulled my Jeep out of the garage tonight—a vehicle I hadn't driven in months. The top is down and the salty ocean air is blowing through Mia's chestnut hair as we cruise down the Pacific Coast Highway. She's dressed in cutoff jean shorts, sandals and a peach-colored T-shirt. She looks cute and at least ten years younger than her thirty years. I have a ball-cap pulled over my eyes and am similarly dressed in shorts and a T-shirt. It feels damn nice to be out of the suit and tie I wear every day.

'Almost there,' I say, as I slow and pull off into a parking area. Mia's eyes light up as she realizes where we're going. 'Have you been to the Santa Monica Pier before?' I ask.

'No,' she says, her eyes growing wide as she takes in the view.

'Come on, you're going to love it.'

We exit the car, and I take her hand, guiding her toward the sights and sounds that await. The giddy stride to her step and the smile that's yet to fade tells me that this date is much more her type of fun.

As we walk along the beach, the pier looms in the distance, and her eyes are drawn to the huge Ferris wheel at the end of the pier that overlooks the blue water below. I'd seen an old photograph of the ride cut from a magazine and glued onto a page in her scrapbook.

'Are we going up there?' she points to the top.

'If you like,' I say, my tone neutral. I can't have her knowing how stupidly excited this gets me. 'But first, I thought we'd have a picnic dinner on the beach.' I motion to the backpack slung over my arm.

'It's perfect, Coll.' She lifts up on her toes and plants a kiss on my cheek.

We find a quiet spot, away from the tourists and visitors. From the backpack, I pull out a blanket and bottle of wine. Mia sinks down and digs through the bag, pulling out the rest of the items while I open the wine—she finds two plastic cups, a package of crackers, a block of cheese, fresh berries, sliced lunchmeat and cookies.

'This is amazing. You're the world's best boyfriend.' As soon as she's said it, she slaps a hand over her mouth. 'Sorry.'

'Don't be. Is that what I am to you?'

She nods, slowly. 'I—I think so.'

'Good. You're all I want.' I lean in close and kiss her lips. She tastes like wine and strawberries. It's an intoxicating combination,

133

and I want to feast on her—forget this spread we have laid out before us.

I feel her hand pat my cheek and she pulls away after several minutes. 'We better behave.' Her eyes stray to a small family with young children who are down the beach a little ways.

'Fine,' I grumble.

She laughs at me and pops another berry into her mouth.

'Do you like this date better than going to a designer opening?' I ask.

She removes her sandals and digs her toes into the warm sand and shoots me a daring look. 'What do you think?'

I smile. 'I'll admit, I want to wow you. I guess I may have been over thinking things.'

'You've gotta stop thinking with your head so much.' Placing her palm over my heart, she leans close. 'Everything you need to know is right in here.' She pats my chest gently.

'I'm starting to get that,' I say. Listening to my heart is making more and more sense.

After we finish our meal and the bottle of wine, we head to the pier, feeling happy and slightly tipsy. The flashing lights and cheerful sounds of the carnival games draw us in.

We watch a group of kids play a dancing game for several minutes before Mia announces that she wants me to win her a giant stuffed animal. Rising to the challenge, I strut over to the strong man challenge, pay the operator the five bucks and pick up the heavy mallet. Tossing a flirty grin over my shoulder at Mia, I raise the mallet overhead and slam it down against the target. The game erupts into a fit of lights and sounds, sirens whistle and bells ding. I pull Mia into my arms as the operator hands me my ticket for the prize I've won. 'Let's go get you that stuffed animal.'

'My hero.' She takes my hand and pulls me to the counter where we discover that my big win was not enough to get her the giant teddy bear she wants. The clerk hands her a miniature pig and we both burst into laughter.

'The size is a little disappointing,' she says, turning the tiny stuffed animal over in her hand.

'There's a phrase I've never heard before.' I smirk.

Realization dawns on her and she swats my shoulder. 'You're awfully cocky.'

I shrug and fix a smile on my mouth. 'It's not cocky if it's true.'

'Come on, naughty boy, you promised me a ride on that.' She points straight up to where the Ferris wheel rises overhead.

'Yes, ma'am. Come on.' I lace my fingers in hers and tug her toward the ride.

Seated together in the bucket seat, Mia squeals and tucks herself in against my body as we begin to rise. Once we're at the top, the ride stops, and we enjoy the spectacular view of the sun sinking into the ocean. The moment is perfect and it feels like time has stopped. I love how Mia can turn every day into an adventure and how she's totally down with eating sugary fair foods and cheered on the little ones playing that dancing game. She makes me happy. Her outlook on life is simple and straightforward. She's not at all pretentious or phony. I love how warm and sweet she is.

The light breeze lifts strands of Mia's hair, and as it floats around her face, I place one hand against her neck and guide her mouth to mine. We kiss deeply, our tongues moving together, as a thousand emotions erupt inside of me. One thing becomes abundantly clear: I'm in love with Mia. Maybe I have been all along, but my head is just now figuring out what my heart has always known. My pulse pounds in my ears as the depth of this moment rushes over me. Mia lets out a small moan of pleasure, and I force myself to break the kiss.

'Gremlin…' I growl.

She opens her eyes, lazily, and blinks at me.

'It's time to get home.'

She can hear the desire in my rough voice, and she nods twice.

When the ride comes to a stop, I help her off, and we hurry back to the Jeep. I need her like I've never needed anyone.

Mia pushes her hands into my hair and leans up on her toes to kiss me. Taking firm hold of her wrists, I remove them from my hair and bind them behind her back, which makes her breasts jut out. 'Undress and wait for me on the bed,' I growl.

She whimpers, but as soon as I release her, she does as I've instructed, removing her clothing piece by piece while I watch. We are each learning each other's sexual tastes and fantasies. She likes it when I take charge. I make her wait, turning and heading into the closet where I pull off my T-shirt and toss it into a basket. When I emerge with my shorts unbuttoned, and riding low on my hips, Mia's eyes grow wide. She's lying on her side in the center of the bed, waiting for me, just as I knew she would be.

'Beautiful,' I whisper, laying down behind her and running my fingertip along her spine. When I reach the top of her ass, she shudders and pulls in a breath. 'Shh,' I admonish. 'I'm in charge, remember?'

She squirms on the bed, ready for more contact, but I won't give it to her, not yet anyway.

'Tell me what you want,' I whisper, placing my lips at the base of her neck.

'You,' she breathes.

'You have to do better than that.'

'This,' she says, pushing her ass back to grind against my erect cock.

The lush curve of her soft ass pressing against me feels incredible. I'd be content to just lay here and let her work herself against me, but I know we're both craving more. I lift her top leg and place it over mine, opening her to my liking.

'Are you wet for me already?' I ask.

We'd made out heavily in the Jeep—with her grinding in my lap—before we drove home. Putting her in her own seat and buckling her up was one of the hardest things I've ever done. I wanted to take her hard and fast, not giving a single fuck that we were in a parking lot for an amusement park. Luckily, common sense won out.

Mia moans and reaches between us to stroke me, touching the head of my cock to her opening so I can feel just how ready she is for me. The hot, pleasurable sensation cuts through me like a knife.

Goddamn.

I growl out a curse as she uses her own moisture to rub me from base to tip.

Planting a damp sucking kiss at the base of her neck, I press my hips forward, stimulating her clit with the head of my dick. 'Are you ready for me?'

'Please,' she cries.

Easing myself in behind her, I give her everything she's asked for.

Chapter Twenty-Two

Mia

I can hardly believe three whole months have passed since I surprised Collins by showing up on his doorstep with almost everything I owned. It's even harder to believe how things have turned out since then.

Collins and I share the master bedroom. We have for a few months. It still feels a bit odd to have so much space just for a room to sleep in, but when I pointed this out to Collins, he got a smug grin on his face and grumbled that he planned on doing a whole lot more than just sleeping with me in this room. He'd definitely delivered on that promise.

Saturdays Collins and I usually spend the day together, however, today he has some loose ends he has to tie up at work, so we won't be meeting up until later.

I lay in bed, still in a lazy Saturday morning haze, when Collins emerges from the bathroom, clean-shaven, wearing jeans and a T-shirt. He sits down next to me on the bed and leans over, brushing a stray hair back from my face.

'I can get up and eat breakfast with you,' I say and start to sit up, but he pushes me back.

'Don't. Stay in bed. I'm running late anyways. I'll eat on the way. Sorry I have to go in,' he says, kissing me gently on the lips.

'It's okay,' I smile, hoping to wash his worry away. 'You've been working hard on this business deal, and I know it means a lot to you. Besides, we still have tonight.'

'Mia, you're too good for me.'

I shake my head. 'Just good enough.'

That gets a smile from him.

'I'll see you later.' He steals one more kiss before rushing out the door.

As I watch Collins go, it hits me how lucky I am to have him. Despite being close to him my whole childhood, our relationship now is on an entirely different level. We connect better emotionally and physically than I ever dreamed. I love him deeply, and though we haven't flat out spoken those words yet, I know we both feel it. I feel it when he holds me close and whispers promises to take care of me. He feels it when he's in the mood to discuss his mother, and I listen patiently and hold his hand. We are there for each other in all the ways that matter.

I hug his pillow to my chest, and breathe in his musky scent that still lingers. He is my rock, my savior, and at times, my comic relief. He's always seen something in me that no one else has. Starting the first day we met. Me, in last year's pants that were two inches too short and a second-hand T-shirt. But Collins didn't see any of that. He saw the girl beneath. My mother said I had a heart of gold, and while my father always warned that it doesn't get you very far in life, Collins saw inside me and he loved all of me, which made me feel whole. I could just be me and not worry that all my classmates had designer clothes, and yet my family scraped by to make ends meet. It never occurred to me that I might not measure up, because to him, I always have.

I stretch one more time and pull myself out of bed. I've got to get ready too. Kylie asked me to go with her and Sophie to get mani-pedis. Although Sophie's pregnancy has been going fine for the most part, apparently her emotions have been a little out of control. Mostly to the effect of her bursting into tears every so often. She swears she's fine, and it's just the hormones, but Kylie thought it would be nice for the three of us to go out and have a girls' day at the salon. Just to lighten up her mood.

Collins has been trying to get me to pamper myself for months now, offering to buy me a spa day. He went on about how I went through some rough times with losing my job. But I'm not comfortable having him spend all that money on me, even if he can afford it.

After showering I head to my enormous new closet. The first time Collins showed it to me I couldn't believe it. There's a chandelier! The thing is larger than my old bedroom was in Connecticut, and entirely too big for the small suitcase worth of clothing I brought here.

Even after I received my settlement money from my last job and bought some new clothes for my job at the law firm, I still only use a small set of drawers in one corner, and a small section for hanging my dresses.

I pull on a tank top and some cutoffs, slip into my flip-flops, grab my keys and purse and head out to meet the girls.

When I arrive at the salon, they are already there.

'Here she is,' Sophie says, her voice is high and excited, and she smiles big. I've only been in LA a few months, but I love how close I've become with Sophie and Kylie already.

I give them both hugs in greeting, and the spa staff set us up in three neighboring pedicure chairs. I try to get Sophie to sit in the middle seat, but she wants to sit near the window, so I end up between the two.

I sink my feet into the hot water, and sigh. It's been a while since I've done something so decadent. I'm used to worrying about rent, or the next student-loan payment. I still have student-loans, but with the salary at my new job, the fact that I no longer pay rent, and the settlement money which I'm mostly saving, I finally have room to breathe financially.

'This is the best,' Sophie says as she sinks back into her chair.

'How's the little one treating you?' I ask eagerly, motioning to her stomach. She isn't showing yet, but there is a glow about her that hints at her pregnancy. I can't help but get excited for her. Just talking about it brings an energized grin to my face.

'Oh just fine,' she rolls her eyes as if it's no big deal. 'I feel almost guilty because I haven't had morning sickness or anything.'

'I bet you can't wait to meet him or her,' I say.

'I am super excited,' she says. A small tear wells in her eyes. A reminder that her hormones are acting up. 'Maybe one day, you and Collins can have a baby too. And if you have one soon, they could play together.' She sniffles, and another tear drifts down her cheek, but then she laughs at herself, making Kylie and I laugh with her.

Yet I realize how envious I am of her. I can't help but wonder and hope that one day Collins and I will have a family of our own. The idea of it is enough to give me a rush of joy. I know Collins would be a great father. My heart warms at the image of him chasing around our little son or daughter, resurrecting the tickle monster just for them.

Of course we still haven't talked about our future, I don't want to rush him. For now I'm happy just being with him. And I know he's happy too.

My phone chirps and I check it to find a message from Collins. *I miss you, Gremlin.*

I smile and show the message to Sophie and Kylie.

'Awe,' Kylie says.

'He can't send you messages like that,' Sophie says. 'Or I'll spend the whole dang day happy crying.'

'Sorry,' I say. I text him back.

Miss you, too.

Can't wait to see you.

Get back to work. The sooner you finish, the sooner we can...

Kylie leans forward in her chair. 'Pace wants us to have one soon too. When I met him, I never would have thought he would be a kids guy, but he's so damn good with Max, I've been pushing him to wait until after we're married, but I kinda can't wait, either.'

'I know,' I say. 'Maybe part of it's being around you two, but I seriously feel like my ovaries are screaming for me to have a baby, and soon.' I feel like I'm admitting too much, but I don't care. Somehow I've already started to think of Sophie and Kylie as sisters, so talking to them like this just feels right.

'I'm sure your turn will come soon,' Kylie says. She raises her eyebrows and smiles knowingly.

I laugh. 'I hope so, but we still haven't talked about marriage.'

Sophie's eyes go wide and she almost jumps out of her chair. 'But you want to marry him, don't you?'

'Of course,' I answer, blushing. I don't say that I'm hoping one day, maybe in the near future, he'll propose to me again. It doesn't even have to be cheesy romantic. He could just poke me hard in the arm again and say he wants me to be his wife. I want to be patient, because I know he needs time to think about things. Collins doesn't make decisions lightly. He's deliberate and thoughtful. Besides, I've only been back in his life a few months. And I'm just happy to be with him. Finally I add, 'He seemed to need some time, so I haven't brought it up again. I'm waiting for him to.'

Sophie relaxes back into her chair, but I realize for the first time that her reaction is slightly melodramatic. I wonder if her hormones are doing this to her.

After the pedicures we move to the nail stations to have our hands done. Through the whole thing, the conversation seems to center on children and family. I'm not sure who's guiding the conversation, as it seems to flow naturally, but the topic fills me with both hope and longing. I can't help but remember how good Collins was with his younger brothers. It fills me with a happy thought for our future.

Just as we're finishing up drying our nails, the door opens and in walks a man, his arms loaded with long stem, red roses. 'Mia Monroe,' he says over his bundle. Shocked I look at Kylie and Sophie. Collins knew I would be out with them today, but I never told him which salon we were going to. Sophie looks sufficiently guilty. She must have clued him in.

With difficulty I accept the bundle of flowers, finding a card inside.

I've got something special planned for tonight. Go with Sophie to Colton's to get ready. I'll meet you there later.

-Collins

I look up at Sophie and notice that the guilt on her face has grown. 'How long have you known about this?' I ask her.

'I plead the fifth,' she says, laughing.

I narrow my eyes at her. 'Do you know what he has planned?'

'It's a surprise. And I'm pregnant, so don't get any ideas about trying to torture it out of me.' She cradles her stomach with one arm.

I laugh.

We say goodbye to Kylie who has to pick up Max from a play-date, then the delivery guy helps me load the roses into my car and I follow Sophie over to her and Colton's house.

We pull into the circle drive up front and head inside and up to the second floor. She leads me into a guest suite and has me take a seat at the dressing table. As I settle in I can't help but get excited watching Sophie rush about. She darts into the small walk-in closet, only to reemerge with a bottle of champagne in one hand and a silk, lavender dress hanging over the other.

'Put this on,' she says, hanging the dress on the closet door, then turning her attention to the bottle of champagne.

The dress is beautiful. It's long and flowing, and yet the cut is simple. I skim my fingers along the fabric. It's so smooth, and my absolute favorite shade of purple. I pull off my tank top and shorts and pull the dress on, noticing as I zip it up that it fits like a glove.

'How does he know my dress size?' I ask as I step in front of the mirror, admiring how well it hugs my every curve.

Sophie hands me a glass of champagne, and looks with me at my reflection in the mirror. A single strap wraps around my neck, allowing for a modest v-neck front. The back is low, looping down almost to my waistline.

'Perfect,' Sophie says. 'It's the perfect Mia dress.'

She's right. I turn in the mirror, admiring myself. 'How did he know?'

There's a knock at the door, and Sophie winks at me before rushing to answer it.

I continue to stare at my reflection in the mirror, still amazed at how much I love the dress with its long flowing skirt.

'You can set up over here.' Sophie's voice pulls my attention to where she's letting in two women I've never seen before who are loaded up with cases that look like toolboxes.

'What is this?' I ask. Now I know Collins has gone overboard.

'This is Nicole and Stella. They're doing your hair and makeup for tonight.'

My mouth drops open. 'I don't believe it,' I say. 'Collins has lost it. I know how to do my own makeup and hair.'

'Humor him tonight. He said he wanted to pamper you this once. Just let him have his way.' Sophie says.

I smile. 'I guess I don't have a choice. What Collins wants, Collins gets.' I sit down in an exaggerated huff at the dressing table.

Yet it's hard not to sit up straight and feel the rush of excitement that Collins put all this thought and care into something for me.

I take a sip of my champagne and watch as the stylist sets up her equipment around me.

'Right, I'll see you in a bit,' Sophie says by the door.

'Where are you going?' I ask.

'I have to get ready, too.' She smiles and then slips out, shutting the door behind her.

Chapter Twenty-three

Collins

I'm sitting in Colton's library, having a drink with my brothers at a time I thought would be filled with anticipation. Instead, I find our conversation is giving me a headache. I swirl the liquor in my glass, wondering if I'm making a mistake. Everything about this has felt right, but their reactions are making me question myself.

'So you've planned an entire wedding, and you never even asked her to marry you?' Pace asks, chuckling at me from behind his fist, like this is the goddamn funniest thing he's ever heard.

Colton stares at me, wide-eyed in a rare display of bewilderment, waiting for me to answer. As if he hasn't been here with me the last few weeks helping me plan the whole damn thing.

'Basically,' I say. *I'd asked her twenty years ago. That counts, right?* I orchestrated her outing with the girls, and have caterers' and designers downstairs readying Colton's house as we speak.

'You've gone all bat-shit crazy on us, haven't you,' Colton says, snapping out of his stony silence.

'I gave her my word when we were ten years old. I'm just making good on my promise,' I say.

'Is she going to freak out?' Pace asks.

'I don't know.' I don't think so. I guess some part of me knew from the day she showed up on my front porch—looking small and scared—that inviting her in would lead to this. Her in a wedding dress. Me in a tux. My brothers at my side. 'Text Sophie, ask how it's going upstairs,' I say to Colton.

Colton looks down at his phone and chuckles.

'What?' I ask, my stomach turning with nerves for the first time since I planned all this.

'Sophie says the hardest part is that the pregnancy has made her so emotional, she keeps crying, but so far Mia doesn't suspect anything. She says Mia is going to make a beautiful bride.'

I have no response, because when I picture Mia in that custom-made silk dress, my mouth gets dry and a lump forms in my throat. I'd taken the idea from *The Gremlin Files*. Somehow, I knew she had to get married in that dress. That lavender silk number is exactly what she's supposed to be wearing today, not some over-done white, poufy thing that I can't get off of her later.

'So you're not nervous at all?' Pace asks.

I take stock of how I feel. Nervous doesn't describe it. I'm excited. And ready. 'Nope,' I answer.

Colton's phone chimes and he looks down at the screen. 'Sophie says Mia's ready.'

The gravity of the moment hits me and I fight off a wave of emotion. I cover a few last minute details with my brothers, discussing the rings with them when a knock at the door surprises us.

Colton answers it, and I see it's my assistant.

'All the guests are here and seated on the beach, sir,' she says.

'It's go time,' Pace says and claps me on the back.

'You ready for this, brother?' Colton asks.

'Fuck yeah,' I say, grinning like a lovesick fool.

Chapter Twenty-Four

Mia

The stylist pulls my hair back in a wavy updo, allowing several loose curls to escape, framing my face. Then she weaves in fresh violets, which match the dress perfectly. The makeup artist takes her time, and when she's finally done, I stand in front of the wardrobe's full-length mirror in shock. My hair, the dress, and my face all blend together so smoothly. I'm not normally one to over think how I look, but I have to admit the woman I see looking back at me is beautiful.

As if on cue, Sophie comes to collect me as soon as my makeover is finished. When she enters the room, I instantly know something is up. She's wearing a deep purple satin dress, and her hair and makeup has been professionally done as well.

'Serious double date,' I say.

She nods and smiles through a faintly blushing face. 'Come on, the guys are waiting.'

I look around the room realizing I'm missing one thing. 'I don't have any shoes that will go with this.'

Sophie's eyes widen and she bites her lip. 'What size shoe do you wear?'

'Eight,' I say.

'You certainly won't fit into my size sevens. It's okay, you can just wear what you came in,' her voice drops as her eyes find my tired flip flops in the corner of the room where I'd kicked them off.

'No. It's fine,' I say and step into them. 'This dress is long enough that no one will see.' I pull my feet under the dress then and show her.

Sophie considers for a moment, then nods. She hooks her arm through mine and guides me downstairs. I assume we'll be heading out front to be picked up by the guys, but she makes an abrupt turn towards the back of the house. Sophie is strangely silent, and won't look me in the eye. When she wipes a tear from her cheek I don't know what to think.

Colton's house is on the ocean, the beach is literally in his back yard. We step out the back to an amazing view of the Pacific. Deep blue water that sparkles from the sun. I have absolutely no idea why Collins would want me to get this dressed up to go run around in the sand, but at least I know why there were no shoes waiting for me.

Kylie meets us at the bottom of the steps. She's wearing a dress that matches Sophie's, and holds a huge bundle of lavender silk in her arms.

My skin prickles with an excited chill, and I notice my heart is fluttering like a hummingbird's wings. Somehow, my body has figured out what's going on, but it's not bothered to tell me. My legs have forgotten how to walk, and Sophie has to help me down the path to the beach.

It's that magical time of day, just before sunset, and rows of chairs fill the beach. The chairs are filled with people all facing Collins, who stands at an altar, flanked by his brothers. When we reach a spot several yards from the ocean, my feet stop again.

'What is this?' I ask, even though I'm pretty sure my slow brain has finally figured it out.

'It's your wedding,' Sophie says. She's crying as she and Kylie work to unravel the large bundle of fabric Kylie's been cradling.

It is, of course, the train for my dress. *My wedding dress.* As they work to attach the train a wave of emotion hits me. I cover my mouth with my hands, unable to speak.

'Don't forget to breathe, sweetie,' Kylie says.

Which is when I notice that, with this surprise, Collins has quite literally taken my breath away.

I manage to pull in a shaky breath while I stand there looking down the aisle at Collins who's eyes have found me and is gazing back. He's traded in the T-shirt and jeans from this morning and now wears a black tuxedo, which even from this distance makes him look so handsome that I ache to be alone with him.

Sophie slides a piece of paper into my hand and my fingers shake as I unfold it and see that it's a note from Collins.

Gremlin,

Some part of me has known all along that you are the one I wanted to spend the rest of forever with. From the first day we met, I've known that you are the one for me. The five-year-old me knew it. The ten-year-old me—the one who thought all girls were gross—knew it.

Every time you smile, I can't help but feel happy with you. The sound of your laughter is a song that has the power to lift my spirit. Your kind soul has guided me through so much.

The day you left when we were teenagers, I thought my life was over, and for a long time, it seemed it was. When you came crashing back into my world, you shook things up so much, at first I didn't know what to think, but now I know what you were doing. You showed me how to live again.

I'm sorry it took so long for the idiot thirty-year-old me to figure it out. But this whole time you've had my heart,

and I hope on this day you'll say yes and agree share your
life with me.
   I love you. I always have, and always will.
   My first. My last. Be mine forever?

-Collins

Halfway through reading the letter my eyes have already blurred with tears.

'Are you okay?' Kylie asks.

In an attempt to process everything that's happening, I blankly nod.

'Good, because it's time.' Kylie squeezes my hand before turning and walking down the aisle.

Sophie gives me a hug and then heads down the aisle herself, followed shortly by Max who carries a small ring bearer pillow. I look into the crowd and see my parents and even Leila and her husband are here. Another wave of joy hits me as I realize he's also done this. He's flown them here just for me. My mom's eyes find mine, and she smiles so big, I feel it deep inside me. It's been three months since I've seen her, and it takes every ounce of self-control I have not to break out into a huge grin and wave frantically at her.

When Max reaches the front, soft music begins, and the crowd stands up, turning to face me. I realize it's my turn, and I'm struck with a wave of sheer panic. I can't believe I really am getting married. Today. Conflicting emotions rush through me. I had no idea this morning that I would be standing here about to get married. A bundle of nerves twists inside me, and I pull in another shaky breath, praying that I don't faint. Oh God, I don't know if I can do this. Everyone is watching me, waiting to see what I'm going to do.

I look up, and when I lock eyes with Collins, the strength and love in his gaze warms me, and my body relaxes. I know this is the right thing. My feet find their purpose, I kick off the flip-flops and I take my first step down the aisle, relishing the feel of sun-warmed sand beneath my feet. The eyes of the crowd are on me, but I'm unable to take my eyes off him—the only man I've ever loved.

When I meet him at the altar, he takes my hands in his and leans in close. The sound of the crashing waves nearby means if we talk softly enough, our guests won't hear us, and gives us a moment of privacy.

'Is this okay?' he whispers, wiping a tear from my cheek with his thumb.

'It's better than I could have ever imagined.' My voice is quiet and a bit shaky, and my vision is blurring again with tears. Collins' eyes fill with concern. I smile through the tears, and try to wipe them away, but it's no use, so I laugh.

At that, Collins' face brightens and he smiles. And I can see from the look in his eyes that he truly does adore me, and there's no place he would rather be.

The official's words are perfect, and I'm surprised to hear him telling the story of us, and the collective chuckle from the guests when he tells them we've been engaged for twenty years. I manage to get my tears mostly under control about halfway through the ceremony, so that when it's time for us to kiss, I'm not a total mess. Collins bends down, taking me in his arms, and I reach my hands around his neck. He presses the sweetest kiss against my lips. It's gentle, slow, and he draws it out, teasing me with little licks from his tongue. His hand brushes the bare skin of my back and I feel him harden against my stomach. It strikes me immediately that fifty or so of our closest friends are watching. We both go rigid and then begin laughing mid kiss, which seems to help his *situation*. He looks down at me through hooded eyes though and grumbles, 'We'll take care of that later,' in a voice low enough that only I can hear.

After the wedding, we take pictures near the surf and then join our guests under a big white tent on the beach behind Colton's house. Collins has thought of everything. There's a beautiful, multi-tier cake with purple flowers, a band playing soft jazz, and, the best part, all of our friends and family.

I find Leila on the dance floor, and join her.

'I'm so glad you came.' I pull her in for a hug.

'You look so happy,' she says, hugging me back 'I'm glad you listened to me.'

I'm not sure if she's talking about our her initial drunken advice that I should come out here in the first place, or her later advice when she encouraged me to stay, but I'm glad I listened to Leila—both times—and I'm glad she was right.

'I told you, you were right,' I say.

She smiles, I know it's something she's been waiting to hear ever since she got here, but her smile also says she's happy for me.

A slow song comes on, and Collins appears at my side and pulls me to him. He's not afraid to dance. At least not with me. We slow dance simply, my arms around his neck and his resting at my waist. Our bodies know each other, so even if we don't know the song, we sway together perfectly.

I feel blessed that I'm able to share the best day of my life with all our loved ones. And I know I'm the luckiest woman alive because the man of my dreams has put this all together for me.

As we dance, my left hand is resting on his shoulder and I admire the way the diamond ring on my finger catches the light. 'I can't believe you did all this,' I say. 'And kept it all a secret.'

'My brothers thought I was a little crazy planning all of this without officially asking you first.'

'It was insane.' I press my lips to his. 'But in the very best way.'

'I love you, Mia,' he says, his voice uncharacteristically thick with emotion.

'I love you, too. Always have,' I admit.

Through the reception Collins doesn't leave my side. His eyes and hands find their way all over my dress, and it's obvious his desire to be alone with me rivals my desire to be with him.

Soon enough Collins announces that it is time for us to leave. As much as I've enjoyed the celebration with everyone, I can't wait to get Collins alone and out of that sexy as hell tux. Our guests throw rice as Collins helps me into the waiting limo. He's refused to tell me anything about our honeymoon other than that we're having one. He also assures me that he's okayed the time off with my employer. The information wins him yet another kiss from me. He has truly thought of everything.

As we near our destination it becomes clear that he can no longer hide his plans from me. We pull into the marina and Collins helps me out, guiding me towards his boat, The Gremlin. As we near the water, I come to a realization and stop. 'We don't have any luggage. I didn't pack,' I say.

Collins ushers me along down the dock. 'What do you think Kylie was doing while you were getting all dolled up? I had her go to our house and pack everything in your closet that wasn't nailed down. Although,' his voice gets raspy and he growls into my ear, 'I plan on keeping you naked for the better part of the next two weeks.'

My panties dampen instantly and a tiny gasp escapes my lips.

Collins chuckles and with little effort whisks me off my feet, making me squeal with surprise. He cradles me in his arms and steps towards the yacht's ramp. 'Collins,' I say nervously, locking my arms around his neck. I'd boarded the boat many times and knew the ramp was sturdy, but worried that with him holding me, we might end up a little too top heavy.

He stops and his eyes lock on mine. 'It's okay, Gremlin. I've got you.' The assurance in his voice reminds me that I have nothing to worry about, because Collins has always protected me. He's never let anything bad happen to me, and never will. I let out a relaxing breath and he continues on board, heading straight down to the lower deck.

He doesn't stop until we're in the master suite with the door closed and locked behind us. Still he doesn't let go of me right away, instead pulling me into a kiss while setting me down gently next to the bed. As he kisses me his hands trace a path down the smooth silk fabric of my gown. He unzips the side zipper and helps me out of the dress, carefully pulling the strap over my head then letting the dress drop to the floor.

The backless dress didn't allow for a bra, so now I stand in front of him wearing my purple lace panties and my flip-flops from earlier in the day. It seems an odd combination to me. I giggle as I kick off the silly beach shoes.

He laughs too as he shrugs out of his jacket and undoes his cufflinks. 'Life will never be boring with you.' He steps forward, letting me help him with the buttons on his shirt.

I'd always thought making love on my wedding night would be a nerve-wracking affair. With Collins I'm not nervous at all, I'm full of excitement, and as we unbutton his shirt we both realize our intense need to be naked and in each other's arms and work faster, finally pulling off his shirt and undershirt.

Faced with his bare chest, my body fills with heat, and desire pools inside me.

'Take off your panties,' he says.

I do as he says, feeling the heat and desire grow as he tells me what to do. I stand fully naked in front of him. His eyes drink in my body. I'm glad I recently waxed, because I know he likes me bare.

'Get on the bed.' His voice is raspy and low. I find just the commanding tone of his voice is enough to make me wet. I sit back on the bed, and move to the center, waiting for him. He knows the wait is torture for me, and he takes pleasure in teasing me this way.

His eyes remain on my body and his hands carefully work at unbuckling his belt. Just watching him work slowly at removing his clothing is enough to make me press my legs together, in need of release.

'Are you ready for me?'

'Yes,' I say.

'Show me.'

I want to show him, but I'm not sure what he wants.

'Touch your beautiful breasts for me while I get undressed. Give me a show.'

I do as he says, cupping my breasts in each hand, pinching my nipples, which are already hard. I pull at them and tease them, and it feels so good I have to squeeze my legs together tighter.

'Open your eyes,' he says, his voice is close.

I hadn't realized I had closed them, and when I open, he's undressed, and lying on the bed next to me. His eyes, still full of desire, lock onto mine. 'I'll take it from here.' His hands cup my breasts, fondling them as he bends down, sucking on each nipple in turn. I arch my back as my body is assaulted with more pleasure than it can handle.

'Are you ready for me?' he asks.

'Yes,' I pant.

His hand slides down over my opening. 'You are so wet.'

'Yes, Collins. I need you. Please.'

He spreads my legs open and kneels down between them, rubbing his tip against my wet flesh. I moan, grab the headboard in anticipation, and he pushes in slowly at first. I've become accustomed to how big he is, but I still need a little time to be able to accommodate his size. He pulls back, then pushes in further, my body taking in more and more with each thrust until he's filled me up, and I have to take a moment to remember to breathe.

'Are you okay?' he asks, his hand cupping my cheek.

After taking another breath, I nod. He leans in, kissing me gently on the lips, then slowly works his hips, and with each thrust I feel the tension build inside me as he moves faster. I find I need and can take more, and I meet his rhythm. He pumps faster and faster, and I want to come, but I wait until he's ready for me. Holding on is torture, but he finally releases me.

'Come for me, Mia,' he says, and I do, in an earth shattering moment of pure bliss, I hold on to him and come apart. He continues pumping and comes just as I'm coming down, pulling me to him, filling me.

After, he wipes me clean, folds me in his arms, and holds me close.

'Mia, my Gremlin, my wife.' He runs his hands through my hair, removing the pins that have held it up all day. 'Mrs. Drake.'

I look up at him and beam at the pride I see in his eyes.

'Collins, my husband.' I trace a line along his smooth abs.

He laughs and squirms as I glide over the ticklish section.

'Was the wedding everything you wanted? Because I know how important it is. Or at least I seem to remember thinking it must be important to you. After all, you started hoarding wedding magazines when you were ten,' he teases.

I bite my lower lip, and look down, embarrassed. But then I answer, 'It couldn't have been more perfect. How long have you been planning this?'

'A little while,' he says, as if it's no big deal.

This morning seems like weeks ago, when he was up early and getting ready to go into 'work.' He must have been preparing all day getting ready. 'How did your business deal turn out?'

'The business deal?'

'The one you've been working so hard on for the past few weeks.' I smile playfully at him.

His lips tug up in a grin. 'So far so good. No, scratch that. It's perfect.'

Epilogue

Pace is in the pool with Max, and Colton is stationed at the grill, cooking succulent pieces of shrimp and steaks, but his eyes keep wandering over to his very pregnant wife.

Reluctant to leave Mia's side, I've been hovering near the lounge chairs where the women are sunning themselves, occasionally fetching drinks, sunscreen and food for their growing bellies.

'I still can't believe we're all pregnant at the same time,' Mia says, placing her hand over her firm, round belly. She looks beautiful, full with my child, glowing and pretty. We had to change up our regular yachting tradition on the weekends since Sophie and Kylie's queasy stomachs didn't tolerate boating. Colton's pool has been well-used this summer.

'I can't believe we're all brave enough to be wearing swimsuits while pregnant,' Kylie laughs. 'Then again, Pace hasn't minded the extra junk in my trunk, he says it's an added bonus.'

I mentally file that under *information I did not need to know about my little brother's ass fetish*. But, damn straight. Because that's the fucking truth.

Sophie shifts, an attempt to get more comfortable and sighs. 'Well, my bikini days are done after today, my top is about to burst open, I'm quite certain of it. And I refuse to buy a bigger size.'

Every time Sophie has to pee, which is about every fifteen minutes, Colton stops what he's doing and hefts her to her feet, where she promptly waddles inside to relieve her over-used bladder. It's actually quite adorable, but when I told her that, she shot me a death glare, so I'm keeping my trap shut.

Mia and Kylie are each about four months along, but Sophie is due any day now. She and Colton are having a little girl, who they plan to name Becca Grace in honor of Sophie's late sister. I think it's a touching tribute. Mia and I talk about names everyday—text them to each other when I'm at work, but so far, we're not sure. I'm guessing once we find out what we're having, it'll make things more clear. We didn't want to waste any time starting our family. We're both thirty, and want to have a few kids—so Mia stopped taking her birth control, and a couple months later—we were expecting.

The women have spent most of this morning talking about their pregnancy woes, a topic which I've become accustomed to in the last several months, but when the conversation around me shifts to pregnancy sex, Mia turns as red as a beet, and I have to excuse myself. There is only so much girl talk I can take. I'll be back to check on them soon, but I need a dose of testosterone before I lose my man card.

I head toward Colton and the appetizing smells emanating from the grill. 'How are they doing?' he asks when I get close.

'Good. But a man can only take so much discussion of food cravings, nipple sensitivity and the best methods for breast feeding.' I shudder.

Colton's eyebrows shoot up, but before he can respond, a burst of laughter drifts over. 'What are they talking about now?'

'Sex,' I say blankly.

Paces wanders over holding Max. They are both wrapped up in beach towels. 'What's so funny over there?' He tips his head in the direction of our women.

'Apparently pregnancy sex,' Colton comments.

Pace frowns and looks over at Kylie. 'I have mixed feelings about the whole thing.'

'What do you mean?' I ask. Lord knows, I haven't been able to keep my hands off Mia. Between her swollen breasts, round hips, and her increased sex drive, we've spent entire Saturdays in bed.

'Dude. I don't want to poke my baby in the head,' he admits.

Colton and I share an amused look, and then break out in a fit of hearty laughter.

Colton removes a shrimp from the grill and blows on it until it's cool, then offers it to Max. 'Here you go, buddy.'

Max babbles something at Colton, then nibbles on his shrimp before toddling over to his mom.

With Max over by the women, Colton thumps Pace on the back of the head. 'Don't be a dumbass, bro. The baby's far away inside the uterus.'

'He's right,' I say. 'There's no way your teeny weeny is going to hurt the baby.'

Pace grunts in disgust. 'Teeny my ass. Step inside that pool house boys, and I'll show you what a real man looks like.'

'No thanks,' Colton says, rolling his eyes. 'My point is that your woman has needs. Needs that you would be fulfilling if you weren't such a pussy,' Colton finishes and turns back to the grill.

'Pregnancy hormones increase the libido,' Colton says.

'Indeed,' I confirm, nodding while Colton and I share a fist-bump. Apparently Mia and I aren't the only ones humping like bunnies these days. Good to know.

'Lunch is almost ready, do you want to gather the women and children?' Colton asks.

Crossing the stone patio together, Pace picks up Max, while I offer to help Sophie to her feet. 'Ready?' I ask her.

She nods and holds out her hands to me. 'Thank you, Coll.'

'Anytime.' I wait while Mia rises to her feet and slips into her sundress. 'Ready for lunch?' I ask, before pressing a kiss to her lips.

'Absolutely. It smells amazing.'

When we're all seated at the outdoor dining table, that Colton has designed to accommodate multiple highchairs, we clink glasses, toasting to family, health and safe deliveries of all three babies.

'So will Dad be flying into town soon?' I ask, after swallowing a bite of steak. He's been here several times in the past few months, meeting Kylie and his first grandson after she and Pace got engaged, and again for my wedding, and then Pace's wedding, which happened a few weeks later.

'Yeah, he flies in on Tuesday,' Colton says.

Sophie places her hand on top of her belly. 'Hopefully I can make it that long.'

We all smile politely at her, and Colton kisses the top of her head. She's been convinced she was in labor three times now.

'You'll be great,' Kylie encourages. 'Just get the drugs,' she says with a wink.

I see Mia cutting her food into small bites.

'Are you getting enough to eat?' I ask, feeding her a bite from my plate.

'I'm getting plenty,' she smiles at me.

I kiss her hand and give our baby a gentle pat. My brothers are used to seeing me act all mushy by now, and they rarely complain. Shit, they're in the exact same boat.

It's crazy that what started as three brothers whose idea of relationships was a one night stand with no commitments and no expectations has grown into what will soon be a family of ten. It's kind of astounding when you think about it. Life may not be a fairytale—there are bumps and detours along the way—but I know Mia is my happily ever after. She is my forever.

Acknowledgements

First, thank you to my family, and most especially to my darling husband for supporting me in all that I do. I'm a lucky lady.

Thank you to my dear author friends, and all around rockstars, Rachel Brookes, Emma Hart and Meghan March for your keen eyes and enthusiasm for this story. A bear hug goes to my publicist Danielle Sanchez for your quick responses and imaginative plans for spreading the word about this series. It is wonderful having you on my team!

There have been so many wonderful blogs who've supported me in this journey, and frankly there are way too many to name. But please know that I appreciate everything you do, for your love of books, for your shameless pimping and for your abundance of love for indies. We couldn't do it without you.

Most of all, thank you to the readers. I heart each and every one of you. Thank you for following this series to the end. I love the Drake brothers, each in their own special way.